Lauren likes Charlie.

Does he like her too?

Lauren's Beach Crush
by Angela Darling

SIMON SPOTLIGHT
New York London Toronto Sydney New Delhi

SIMON SPOTLIGHT
An imprint of Simon & Schuster Children's Publishing Division
1230 Avenue of the Americas, New York, New York 10020
Copyright © 2013 by Simon & Schuster, Inc.
Text by Sarah Albee
Designed by Dan Potash
All rights reserved, including the right of reproduction in whole or in part in any form.
SIMON SPOTLIGHT and colophon are registered trademarks of Simon & Schuster, Inc.
For information about special discounts for bulk purchases, please contact Simon & Schuster Special
Sales at 1-866-506-1949 or business@simonandschuster.com.
Manufactured in the United States of America 0413 OFF
First Edition 10 9 8 7 6 5 4 3 2 1
ISBN 978-1-4424-8036-0 (pbk)
ISBN 978-1-4424-8038-4 (hc)
ISBN 978-1-4424-8040-7 (eBook)
Library of Congress Catalog Card Number 2012950722

LAUREN SILVER FROWNED AND ABSENTLY CHEWED the eraser on her pencil, peering down at the multiple choice test in front of her. Was the answer *A* or *B*? Or even *C*? She felt so unprepared. Like one of those bad dreams where you walk into class and the teacher puts a test in front of you and you realize you are totally clueless. This was so unlike her. She almost always aced tests.

She took a deep breath and cleared her mind, and circled *B* with confidence.

With all the questions answered, Lauren went back and carefully scored herself against the answer key. When she saw the result, she couldn't help but smile.

She'd been right all along. She was meant to be with Charlie Anderson!

The test she took was called "Is He Your Soul Mate?"

She had come to rely on the monthly tests in her *Chic Chick* magazine for guidance on all things related to Charlie Anderson. When this month's issue came out and Lauren saw the title of the quiz, she hoped deep down that it was a sign. Now that she'd taken—and aced—the test, she *knew* it was a sign.

Was Charlie Anderson her soul mate? Yes he was.

She lay back on her bed and whispered his name out loud, slowly, dreamily—Charlie Anderson. It had such a perfect sound to it. The "ch" of Charlie, then the "-arlie," the three-syllable last name a lilting triplet, the first and last names just right together. Like a little song. It was the perfect name for the perfect boy.

In the margin of her magazine she doodled in large loopy letters. "Lauren Anderson." Then: "Lauren & Charlie." "Charlie & Lauren." They sounded like a couple. Their names just fit together so perfectly. As if it was meant to be. Because, of course, it was. Lauren & Charlie TLF. True Love Forever.

She stood up and moved to her desk and opened the drawer, then pulled out the oversize pink index card that was face down and shoved toward the back. She turned it over and studied it.

THE LOVE PLAN:

OPERATION CELL PHONE

She'd drawn a neat flowchart, just as they'd learned to do in science class last spring. Arrows pointed from one box to another: If yes, go to this box. If no, go to that box. They all ended up at the heart-shaped goal at the bottom:

Charlie + Lauren = TLF

Lauren loved plans. She loved organizing things and making lists and having everything in place just so. Her mom joked that it was because she was an only child and liked things the way she was used to them, but her dad told her that it was because she was just like him. They were both "very precise" he said. But being an only child did help. There was no one there to mess up her room or to make her parents veer off schedule. It was always calm and quiet at Lauren's house, and she liked it that way. She'd been to friends' houses where it was total chaos, and she didn't know how they lived with that. Her one friend Padma had two younger brothers and a little baby sister, and there was so much yelling and noise that Lauren sometimes made excuses not to go when she was invited there.

It was Dad who taught Lauren about plans. They

always had a plan in their family. For cleaning out the basement, for juggling the chores, or for their summer vacation, which was starting today with three weeks at the beach. Lauren's dad had mapped out the plan, which he called "Operation Get out of Town," and they'd both been packed and ready to go for days. Lauren knew that at exactly three o'clock Dad would be in the driveway with the car all packed up, waiting for her mom, who would be running around making sure that all the appliances were turned off and that the plants were watered. Mom was less of a planner and more "fly by the seat of her pants." Or at least that's how Dad described her.

But Lauren was just like her dad, so she was a planner for sure. And she had a plan of her own this year. It was called the Love Plan, and no one else knew about it.

Lauren's Love Plan was foolproof. It was how she was going to get Charlie to notice her. Then talk to her. And once he did, she knew he would then realize that they were meant to be together. She'd spent months figuring out every angle and anticipating every scenario. There were times Lauren worried that the Plan wouldn't work, or, if it did and Charlie noticed her, that he wouldn't like her after all. Lauren knew she was nice and everything, but she wasn't the most popular girl in the school or the class president or anything like that. She was just normal. But Mom always told her she was a "good soul" and Dad always praised her "kind heart." And, according to Mom and Dad at least, those things were way more important than perfect looks or being the head cheerleader.

It wasn't that Lauren didn't have any friends; she did. She got invited to plenty of sleepover parties and she had a group to sit with at lunch. But when it came down to it Lauren was pretty shy, and since she was used to being by herself a lot, she didn't mind it at all. She could happily read a book in her room or go for a walk by herself. Mom always praised her "independence," but deep down Lauren sometimes worried that she should have one really close friend by now—a BFF. Most of the other girls at school seemed to have one or even two BFFs. A BFF, Lauren thought, sounded really cool. A BFF would be someone she could talk to about the Love Plan.

The first step of the Love Plan meant that Lauren would be starting out her summer vacation by making sure that Charlie had her telephone number. Operation Cell Phone would take care of that. By the end of the summer, when Charlie had fallen totally in love with Lauren and it was time to say good-bye, Charlie would grab Lauren's hand, look deep into her eyes, and say, "Of course I'll be keeping in touch. I've got your number . . ."

She sighed, thinking about how perfect it would be.

"Lauren! Have you eaten breakfast?"

Her mother was calling her from downstairs. Lauren could hear the exasperation in her tone, even from that far away. Quickly she slid the card into the side flap of her backpack, which was sitting on her desk alongside the how-to book she'd ordered online. It was called *Frisbee: Techniques and Tactics*. "I'm coming!" she called down.

"Good! Finally! Come on downstairs. I have a surprise to tell you about!" Lauren was curious. Normally she did not like surprises.

Lauren stood up, catching a glimpse of herself in the mirror over her dresser, and sighed. She wished she would have her growth spurt already. She was practically the smallest girl in her grade, which wasn't such a big deal, but Lauren was pretty sure that Charlie was taller than any of the boys at her school. *Focus on the positive,* Lauren reminded herself. She'd read a whole article in *Chic Chick* about the importance of capitalizing on your assets. She looked at herself carefully and tried to identify her assets, just like the article had said. Everyone said she had a nice smile. And her new haircut made her hair swing and fall over her eyes when she moved her head just so. (Kendra, her haircutter, totally understood the way her hair worked and could practically make miracles happen with her scissors!) Lauren had been practicing tossing her hair a little and had gotten pretty good at it. And, also in the positive column, there was her cute new two-piece bathing suit that she'd spent a big chunk of her babysitting money on last week. She hoped Charlie liked the color, a sort of coral pink. She moved closer and sighed, squinting at her face in the mirror. She had nice long eyelashes, and her older cousin Brit had once told her that her eyebrows had "the perfect natural arch." But there wasn't much she could do about her freckles, besides try to hide them behind her huge sunglasses. Or who knew? Maybe Charlie liked freckles.

"Laur-*en*!"

"Yep! Sorry! Coming!" she called, and hurried down to the kitchen.

The breakfast stuff was still on the table, and her mom was rummaging through a cupboard, searching for the lid to a plastic container. Two bins were on the counter, partially packed with food and kitchen stuff. "Daddy went out and got bagels this morning," came her mother's muffled voice from inside the cupboard. "Have a glass of milk with yours—we need to use it up before we go!"

Lauren popped a bagel half into the toaster oven. "So what's the big surprise you want to tell me?" she asked her mom, opening the fridge and pulling out the carton of milk.

Her mother backed out of the cupboard, her dark hair tumbling from her ponytail in several strands over her face, triumphantly holding the lid she'd been searching for. She stood up and set it on the counter. Then she turned toward Lauren, her eyes shining. "Well," she said, her voice brimming with enthusiasm. "I thought you might be pleased to know that we are bringing someone with us to the beach house this time."

"Oh!" said Lauren, pouring herself a tall glass of milk. "Is Grampy coming to stay with us again? That's fine. I can sleep on the cot on the screen porch."

Her mother shook her head. "Not Grampy. A friend. A friend of yours."

"Of mine?" Lauren set down the carton and furrowed her brow. "Who?"

"Chrissy!" said her mother. "Chrissy Porter!"

"Wait. What?"

"I know!" said her mother happily. "Her mom and I wanted to surprise you guys! We've got it all worked out. Jean and Scott have to go back to California for a couple of weeks to take care of some business with their old house. Chrissy's big sister, Liz, will be away at camp for the whole month, and they didn't really want to drag Chrissy all the way back to California, so I suggested they leave her here. With us. And that we'd take her with us to the beach and the two of you could share your room and be beach buddies for the next three weeks!"

Lauren opened her mouth and closed it again, unsure of what to say. Chrissy Porter was not part of the Love Plan. Chrissy Porter was not part of any plan.

"Honey? This is okay, isn't it? I thought you and Chrissy were good friends." Her mom's face was the picture of concern.

"Oh no, she is—I mean, we are friends. Chrissy is great. It's not that," said Lauren. Her mind was spinning. "That's awesome. I was just—surprised is all."

Her mother looked relieved. "I'm glad you're glad, honey," she said, opening the large utility drawer next to the sink and rummaging around in it for utensils to pack. "I thought you'd be pleased to have someone to spend time with at the beach. And Jean—Mrs. Porter—was so appreciative. They usually rent somewhere for this time of year too, but because of their trip, they couldn't swing it. She was delighted that Chrissy would get a beach vacation after all."

Lauren nodded numbly, still trying to absorb this news.

Lauren's father's muffled voice called from down in the basement.

"I sent your father down there to find my suitcase," she said. "I'd better go see what's going on."

Her mom headed for the basement, leaving Lauren lost in thought.

Chrissy Porter was coming with them? For the whole three weeks? Lauren felt as though someone had just dumped a bucket of ice water down her back. What was she going to do now?

Leaving her bagel uneaten on the plate, she ran upstairs and into her room. She closed the door and threw herself down on the bed.

This was a flat-out, full-blown disaster.

IT WASN'T THAT LAUREN DIDN'T LIKE CHRISSY.

Chrissy seemed pretty nice. But Lauren didn't know her all that well. Chrissy had moved with her parents from Santa Monica the previous fall. Lauren and Chrissy had been in the same math, Spanish, and social studies classes, and they were definitely friendly and sat at the same lunch table and stuff. But they were hardly BFFs. Lauren's mom loved Chrissy's mom, and they were always "double dating" as Lauren's mom said. Their parents had dinner together practically every Saturday night. Lauren realized that made her mom and Chrissy's mom BFFs.

Why did Lauren's mother have to be so nice all the time? Every Thanksgiving they had at least half a dozen unexpected people at their table. They were those with nowhere special to go, whether it was somebody from the office, or friends of friends they'd just met, or totally random people her mom had met in line at the grocery store who had no other plans. Okay, maybe not the last, but still.

Lauren's mom and Chrissy's mom had met each other at a book club that gathered every other Tuesday night. They'd become pals. Lauren was starting to get a little mad. Just because their moms were great friends didn't mean that Lauren had to be great friends with Chrissy. And even if Chrissy was nice—which she was—that did not necessarily mean that Lauren wanted to spend every moment of her three-week vacation with her! And share a room with her. And probably have her around like every second of every day.

And, most importantly, how on earth would she execute the Love Plan with Chrissy hanging around?

"Easy does it, Lauren," she said to herself softly. "This is not necessarily the end of the world."

But she knew it was. Because in truth, Lauren had spent pretty much the entire school year telling all of her friends and anyone else who seemed willing to listen that she and Charlie Anderson were already going out. Which wasn't exactly totally true. In fact, it wasn't even a tiny bit true. The truth was, they had only spoken once, for exactly thirteen seconds.

It had been on a hot day last summer, two weeks into their stay at the beach house. Lauren had been out shopping with her mom. After a day of dragging her around to boring antique stores, Lauren's mom took pity on her and let her go get an ice cream at Rudy's by herself while she finished up shopping across the street. Instead of getting a cone, Lauren ordered her favorite drink—a strawberry frappé with whipped cream. When her order came up, the girl behind the counter called, "Strawberry frappé with whipped!" and Lauren jumped up to get it and practically collided with Charlie, who she'd been crushing on from afar for two straight summers. It turned out, they had both ordered the same thing! He'd been sitting with his friends, around the corner at the long table. Lauren almost couldn't believe it. He loved strawberry frappés with whipped just as she did! What were the odds of that? It had to be a sign.

After a brief, semi-awkward moment when the girl had apologized to them for not realizing it was two separate orders and went off to whip up a second frappé, Lauren and Charlie actually spoke. Their one and only conversation. It went like this:

Lauren: "Small world, right?"

Charlie: "Right."

Lauren: "Um, they sure have awesome frappés here! They're all really good, but strawberry's definitely the best, don't you think?"

Charlie: "Yeah, they're awesome."

Then Charlie stared out the window and waited for the second frappé. Lauren racked her brains trying to come up with something else to say, but it was like she had suddenly lost the power of speech. After an eternity the girl slid the second frappé across the counter for Charlie. Lauren awkwardly lifted her cup in a good-bye gesture and left the shop so Charlie wouldn't see her sitting by herself at a table and think she had no friends. She drifted down the block, barely seeing the world in front of her, playing and replaying the conversation in her mind and visualizing his perfect face. The way one side of his mouth lifted in that lopsided grin he had. The way his light, bright blue eyes stood out against his perfect tan skin. The way his sun-bleached blond hair looked so adorably shaggy. She'd been so distracted thinking about Charlie that she'd almost walked into a parking meter.

And that was the only conversation she'd ever had with him. But even though they had only spoken once, she felt she knew him. After all, she'd been watching him for two summers now. She knew he had a mom and dad and older sister. She knew there was a grandmother in the mix. She knew roughly where his summer house was situated even though she wasn't sure exactly which one it was—right near the beach, one of a clump of houses overlooking the dunes. It wasn't that she was spying on him exactly. Well maybe a little. But Lauren preferred to think of it more as "collecting evidence." Knowing details about him helped when she was formulating the Plan.

But that wasn't all she knew about Charlie. She had observed him many times with his parents at the beach, staring around the side of her book or magazine, her gaze camouflaged behind her big sunglasses. She knew a lot about his family. His dad was tall and handsome for an old guy—no surprise there, given how handsome Charlie was. His mom was blond and pretty, with a cool haircut and expensive-looking sunglasses. She seemed to really like water, because she was always carrying around an enormous bottle of it. Lauren had only seen Charlie's sister a couple of times. The first time had been at the beach last summer. For a sickening moment, Lauren thought she was Charlie's beautiful girlfriend, but then she noticed the family resemblance and relaxed. One day Lauren watched as Charlie threw sand all over his sister and she ran around shrieking and yelling at him. Charlie yelled back and moments later his sister stomped off. The next time Lauren saw them on the beach, they seemed to be fine with each other. Lauren wondered if this was the way brothers and sisters acted all the time, teasing each other and arguing, but then acting later like nothing was wrong. She didn't necessarily want a brother or sister, but she was always curious about what it must be like.

Knowing everything there was to know about Charlie was a big part of the Plan. Thinking of the Plan again, Lauren felt a knot form in her stomach. How would Chrissy respond when she discovered Lauren had lied about her relationship with Charlie? Worse yet, how could she possibly execute the Plan with Chrissy around for the whole trip? Lauren groaned again and fell back onto her pillow, squeezing her eyes closed. Disaster.

And then she heard the doorbell ring. "Lauren," her mother called, practically singing. "Chrissy's here!"

She sat up. She had to act normal, natural. She had to feel out Chrissy, figure out how she might react. Should Lauren even mention Charlie? Should she just avoid the subject entirely? Maybe Chrissy wouldn't remember any-thing about Charlie. Maybe once they got to the beach, she could separate herself from Chrissy somehow and launch a revised version of the Plan. Lauren sighed. This is why she hated surprises. All her carefully laid plans . . .

Lauren tried to put on a cheerful face as she went downstairs. Chrissy was standing in the front hall next to her mom, a large rolling suitcase and a smaller duffel at her feet. Chrissy squealed with delight and threw her arms around Lauren, hopping up and down with excitement. Chrissy was like that. Enthusiastic and bubbly. Lauren had to admit, it was hard not to feel happy around her.

"My mom accidentally spilled it and told me last week!" she said, her long auburn hair bouncing, her big brown eyes sparkling. Chrissy had a backpack slung on one shoul-der and was leaning sideways a little under its weight.

Lauren wondered what was in there. Books? Makeup? The summer math packet? She wasn't really sure what Chrissy was into. Lauren knew Chrissy was smart and that she got good grades. She was also a good gymnast. But what else? What if Chrissy was really into clog dancing or antique quilt collecting or something else Lauren didn't know a thing about?

She realized Chrissy was talking to her.

"I've been bursting to text you to talk about what to pack and everything, but our moms wanted it to be a surprise so I couldn't. Were you so, totally, surprised?"

"Totally," said Lauren, hoping her voice sounded sincere. Of course, she had been surprised, that was for sure.

"Why don't you bring Chrissy up to your room to help you bring down your stuff?" suggested Lauren's mom. "Your dad wants to be on the road in an hour or so to get ahead of rush hour traffic. And you know how he gets with his plans." Yes, Lauren thought. She certainly did.

Chrissy followed Lauren upstairs. Lauren realized with a start that Chrissy had never seen her room. It was weird—they knew each other from school, but this was a totally different situation. Having someone see your room for the first time was always a little stressful. You could tell a lot about a person by looking at her stuff. What if Chrissy didn't like what she saw? Worse yet, what if she said something rude about Lauren's room and her decorating taste? This could be a long three weeks.

They walked in and Lauren darted a look around, trying to see her room with new eyes. One wall was covered in torn-out magazine pages, inspirational sayings, and a few posters of boy bands and her favorite actor from a show about teen vampires. She'd recently talked her mom into repainting her room from the little-girly pink to her favorite shade of purple. Her bedspread had a black and purple pattern on it that Lauren loved. The bookshelf was crammed with books, and there were more stacks of books lined up on the floor in front of the bed. Lauren loved to read, and it wasn't unusual for her to read up to three books in a week, especially during the summer. Her favorite books were mysteries. Would Chrissy think she was too much of a bookworm?

Chrissy threw herself backward on the bed, bouncing up and down a little. "You have an awesome room!" she said. "I love all the purple!"

Lauren smiled with relief and relaxed a little.

"I'm pretty much ready to go," said Lauren, moving to her dresser and collecting the plastic zipper bag full of shampoo, lotion, and hair accessories. She looked at her packing list and checked all of them off. "Okay, that's the last of it."

Chrissy sat up and drew her knees under her chin, hugging her legs and giving Lauren a sly look. "So . . .

are you totally psyched to see Charlie again? Do you guys have a plan to meet the second we get there?" Then she lowered her voice and asked in a dramatic stage whisper, "Do your mom and dad know all about him, or do we have to keep it a secret?"

So much for Chrissy not remembering about Charlie. "Um, not—no. Not exactly," Lauren stammered. She could feel her heart beating fast in her chest. And from the warm feeling on her cheeks, she realized that her face had probably turned beet-red, which had the charming effect of making the freckles sprinkled over the bridge of her nose stand out all the more.

The sly smile fell from Chrissy's face as she watched Lauren's transformation, and she immediately looked concerned. "Should I not have brought him up? I'm sorry! Is everything all right between you two? You didn't, like, break up, did you?"

"No! No, of course not," said Lauren hastily. Then she thought again. Maybe she should tell Chrissy they had broken up, and that she never wanted to talk about Charlie again. They'd have to avoid him for the entire vacation. But then she'd have to abandon the Love Plan. And wait a whole year before she saw him again.

She felt her eyes grow hot. She was not going to cry! That was absolutely positively not going to happen.

"Sorry, Lauren. I didn't mean to upset you!" Chrissy looked even more concerned and a dark cloud of worry passed over her pretty face. "I'm really sorry if I said something wrong . . ."

Lauren turned her back on Chrissy, clutching the edge of her desk. What should she do? Her mom always said that she couldn't go wrong telling the truth. But what if she told Chrissy and Chrissy thought she was an awful liar? And they still had to spend another three weeks together. Lauren gulped.

"Okay, I have to tell you something," she said in a low voice. She walked over to her door and closed it quietly to make sure her parents couldn't overhear them.

"What?" asked Chrissy breathlessly.

"It's a huge secret I haven't told anyone. Not even my mirror. Do you swear to keep a secret?"

"Swear," said Chrissy with a solemn expression as she used her finger to draw an imaginary X over her heart. Chrissy slid her knees down and sat on the edge of Lauren's bed, regarding her with a serious, *you-can-trust-me* expression.

"I . . . I . . . I am a little embarrassed about this," said Lauren.

"You don't have to be embarrassed about anything!" said Chrissy. "After all, we're going to be living together for the next three weeks."

I know, Lauren thought miserably to herself.

"Well, I, um, I kind of exaggerated a little about Charlie."

"You mean he's not as cute as the lead singer of the Flaming Hearts?" laughed Chrissy. "That's okay. I never would have held you to that!"

"No, it's not that. He actually is that cute. Cuter, in fact," said Lauren with a shaky smile. "The thing is, I exaggerated about us. Well, about our relationship."

"Oh, that's okay!" said Chrissy. "My sister always tells me that girls always think it's more serious than boys do. It happens to her all the time!"

Lauren was flustered but she went on. "No, it's . . . well . . . Okay we're not exactly going out."

"Oh, so you're just like friends but it might be more?" asked Chrissy. "That happens to my sister too. All of her boy friends are in love with her actually. They always think their friendships are more than they are. But one of them totally turned into her boyfriend. So it can happen!"

Chrissy was not making this easy.

"We aren't, um, actually, never were . . . We aren't friends. I just kind of know him to say hi to." She paused. "But I have a major crush on him and . . . well, I really want to go out with him!"

That was that. The words were out there. They hung in the air between the two girls. Lauren flinched, waiting for Chrissy to laugh at her. Or to look at her like she was crazy. Or to whip out her phone and text everyone from school with the news.

But she didn't. She smiled. "Okay. Well. So you like him. You have a major crush on him. And you just need to get to know him a little better," she said, a merry gleam in her bright eyes. "Sounds like we have a little project for this vacation!"

Lauren felt the relief wash over her. Could it really be this easy? "Thanks for not being mad," she said, feeling a rush of gratitude toward Chrissy.

"Mad? Why would I be mad?"

Lauren shrugged shyly. "Because of how much I talked about him all year," she said. "I mean, I lied about it."

Lauren felt uncomfortable for a second. What if

Chrissy had suspected all along that Lauren was making it up?

"Whatever," Chrissy said, waving her hand. "And you didn't really lie! You just, well, embellished a little, right?"

"I guess," said Lauren. "I mean I really embellished, though. But I have a plan!"

"What kind of plan?"

Lauren felt encouraged. Chrissy was responding better than she thought she would. Maybe Chrissy could even help her with the Plan. She was going to tell her everything.

"A big plan," Lauren said in a dramatic voice. She sat down next to Chrissy on the bed. "A foolproof way to get him to realize that he and I are made for each other. It's called . . ." Lauren stopped. It seemed silly saying it out loud. "Um . . . I've been calling it the Love Plan. But the main part of it is Operation Cell Phone. And, if executed properly, it will not only result in us talking, but it will also give him my number so he can call me and ask me out after he realizes we're meant to be. I have it planned out step by step. I know we'll hit it off and that he'll instantly realize we're soul mates. At the end of the summer, he will have my number and we can call and text all year until we see each other again next summer."

"Wow, that sounds awesome," said Chrissy, nodding enthusiastically.

The girls sat there for a moment, not knowing what to say next.

"So, what do you know about him, besides the fact that he's gorgeous and that you guys are soul mates?" asked Chrissy.

"Well, he's very athletic, for sure. But I know he's really smart too. I've seen him reading some seriously heavy-duty novels at the beach. And he's really into nature and the environment. I saw him walking around in the dunes one day last summer. I'm pretty sure he was looking for garbage to pick up. And I think he might be part of the Youth Conservation Core, because those are the only people allowed to walk in the protected areas of the dunes."

"Awesome!" said Chrissy. "He sounds amazing. He must—"

"Oh and also?" gushed Lauren. "He loves little kids, just like I do! I mean, how often does that happen, that a boy our age also loves little kids? I know it sounds too good to be true, but I totally saw him playing at the beach last summer with three little kids. The kids were climbing all over him. He was like, totally sweet with them."

Chrissy giggled. "He does sound awesome."

"I know," agreed Lauren.

"Is he our age?"

"I'm pretty sure he's a year older, going into eighth. But I'm not positive. Last summer he was already a lot taller than me. I think he's taller than most of the boys at school." Lauren's face clouded. "You won't tell anyone at school, will you? About how I—um, embellished?"

Chrissy stood up and patted her shoulder. "Your secret is totally safe with me. And I'll help with the plan! So by the time we get to school we won't have a secret because you'll really be Charlie's girlfriend!"

Charlie's girlfriend. Lauren couldn't believe how perfect that sounded.

"So how about you?" asked Lauren eagerly. "Do you have a crush?"

Chrissy nodded and sat back down. "I didn't talk about him much at school, but yeah, I do. His name is Justin. He's back in Santa Monica, at my old school.

We used to take piano from the same teacher and we'd see each other before and after lessons, and at recitals. I had the hugest crush on him forever, and then a few months ago I got up the nerve to text him on his birthday. And he texted me back, and we've been e-mailing and texting ever since. So I think we're actually boyfriend and girlfriend now!"

"That's awesome," breathed Lauren. Chrissy had with Justin exactly what Lauren planned to have with Charlie!

"It's not like we're going out exactly. I was really hoping I'd be able to see him this summer, that I could go back there with my parents, but they said it was too expensive to fly." She sighed. "It's not like I could tell them that I needed to see Justin, so I just had to accept it. I was so upset! Coming to your beach house was like the only good news I've had in ages."

Lauren wondered for a bit why Chrissy had kept Justin a secret from everyone at school. But then she realized that there were some things you just didn't want to share with everyone.

"Girls!" called Mrs. Silver. "We're leaving! Chrissy has to say good-bye to her mom, and you guys have to get all your last-minute packing into the car!"

The girls jumped up. Chrissy helped Lauren by grabbing one of her two small bags, and both raced down the stairs. Plans or no plans, the long anticipated vacation was about to be under way.

chapter 3

THE TRIP WAS SUPPOSED TO TAKE TWO HOURS,
but traffic was bad getting out of the city and it was closer
to three by the time they finally pulled into the shaded,
gravel driveway alongside the brown clapboard house.
Chrissy's eyes widened as she peered out at it from the
back seat.

"Wow," she breathed. "It's so pretty here."

Again, Lauren felt relieved. She thought the house
was pretty, but it wasn't a very large house. And it wasn't
right on the beach. Still, Lauren loved it, and she had been
a little nervous wondering what Chrissy would think of it.
She felt the same amazing feeling she always felt, ever
since her family had bought it as a major fixer-upper from
an elderly lady when Lauren was only five. In the front
yard stood a huge old tree with a knotted rope for climbing. On the side of the house, facing south, orangey-pink

climbing roses grew up a trellis all the way to the roof. As they got out of the car, Lauren could smell the rose-scented, salty sea air.

"Why don't you two bring your things up to Lauren's room? Mom and I will unpack the rest while you give Chrissy a tour, all right?" suggested Mr. Silver.

The girls pulled their suitcases from the mass of stuff in the back of the minivan, and Lauren led the way around to the back of the house, leaning to one side with the weight of her bag, her opposite arm high in the air for balance.

"Here's where we always keep the key," she said, showing Chrissy a loose shingle that swiveled to the side, revealing a key on a hook. She fiddled with the key in the lock and then banged the door open with her hip.

They stepped into the kitchen. It smelled faintly of polish, of the bacon that had been cooked for countless breakfasts over so many years, and ever so slightly musty and damp. Lauren loved this kitchen. The afternoon sunbeams, dancing with dust motes, played across the battered old table in the middle of the floor. They glinted off the gleaming old appliances. There was the old-fashioned mixer on the counter, with which she and her dad had created countless cakes and cookies. She led the way through the kitchen and into the hallway, then up the central staircase to the room at the top of the stairs and on the right.

Lauren's room was bright and sunny, with two twin beds separated by a battered table stacked with Lauren's old books, and gauzy white curtains that billowed in the afternoon breeze. Faded, flowered wallpaper gave it an antique feel that Lauren loved. It had been the same way ever since Lauren could remember, but she always liked it. Lauren realized that no one had ever slept on the spare bed in her room, besides Grampy when he came to stay with them.

"This. Is. Totally. Awesome." said Chrissy, putting down her bags. "It's so great that you don't have to share it with anyone. Well, I mean except for me this summer!" she said, laughing.

Lauren agreed. "Being an only child does have some advantages. We have our own bathroom, too," she said, gesturing to a door off the far end of the room. "Go ahead and unpack if you want, and then we can walk around and I'll show you the town and the beach. It's probably too late for swimming, but my dad says tomorrow is supposed to be a perfect beach day."

Chrissy moved over to the window. "The roses have grown all the way up and around the windows. It's like Rapunzel's tower or something!" she said excitedly, glancing over her shoulder to grin at Lauren. "I'm totally expecting a bluebird to land on the windowsill, or to see Prince Charming down there on a white horse. And look! You can see the ocean from here!" she squealed as she pointed out the window.

"Yep. It's just a two-block walk to our beach. But the one all the kids our age like to go to is a block from town, on the other side. It's called Crane's Beach, and it's literally a five-minute walk from here." Lauren was delighted that Chrissy liked the house, and her room. And she hadn't even seen the beaches yet! Lauren's dad had travelled all over the world for work, but he'd said many times that the beaches around East Harbor were among the most beautiful he'd ever seen.

They both changed into clean shorts and tees. Chrissy scrutinized Lauren's bright pink striped tee and white shorts, and suddenly snapped her fingers. "Oooh, what size shoes do you wear?" she asked Lauren as she knelt and began digging around in her suitcase. Lauren told her and Chrissy grinned. "I knew it—same size as me!" She pulled her hands from her suitcase and Lauren could see she was holding three different pairs of neon rubber flip-flops—green, pink, and yellow. "These were on sale buy-two-get-one-free and so my mom let me get all of them! I'm going to wear the yellow, but do you want to borrow the pink? They would look totally cute with your T-shirt."

Lauren happily kicked off her blue flip-flops and tried on Chrissy's pair. They did look perfect with her outfit. "Are you sure?" she asked tentatively.

"Of course! My flip-flops are your flip-flops!" Chrissy said happily. "This vacation you have doubled your wardrobe!" She giggled. "I take my sister's stuff all the time and she yells at me, but you're welcome to borrow anything."

"Thanks," said Lauren. She looked down at her feet, admiring how nice they looked in Chrissy's shoes. She knew they were just rubber flip-flops . . . so not a big deal . . . but she had never had anyone to share stuff like this with, and it felt really good.

As they headed downstairs, they could hear Lauren's parents unpacking in the kitchen. "Mom! Dad! We're heading out!" called Lauren.

"Where are you going?" asked Mom.

"To show Chrissy the beach and Main Street," said Lauren. "We'll be together."

Mr. and Mrs. Silver exchanged a look, and then Mrs. Silver nodded.

"Take your cell phone with you and be back by seven!" her dad called back. "I'm grilling tonight!"

Lauren grabbed Chrissy's hand and pulled her out of the house before they could change their minds. Having Chrissy here was already a bonus. Normally Lauren wasn't allowed to go anywhere by herself.

"Dad loves to grill," Lauren explained. "Be sure to heap him with compliments about his grilling skills. It will totally make his night!"

"Will do," said Chrissy, giving her a tiny salute.

They turned right, toward town. Lauren's was a sleepy dead-end street with very little traffic. "Our beach is that way," said Lauren, pointing in the other direction, toward the ocean. "It's usually full of little kids because it faces the Sound and doesn't have huge waves. We can check that out later."

Chrissy closed her eyes and breathed deeply. "I love how the air smells like the ocean," she said. "Salty and fishy, but in a good way."

Lauren nodded. She did too. Several seagulls darted above their heads, heading toward the ocean.

After a short walk, turning right and then left, they arrived in the middle of town. "So this is Main Street," said Lauren, sweeping her arm in a *ta-da!* gesture. "It's not a very big town, as you can see, but it gets really crowded in the summer. Main Street goes all the way down to the pier. There are a lot of old houses and antique stores and stuff on the side streets." She shrugged casually. "I can show you those later, if you want." She pretended it wasn't a big deal, because she didn't know if Chrissy liked that sort of thing. Lauren loved the hidden treasures of the town— all the funky old houses, clumped so closely together with "widows' walks" on their top floors. Lauren's mom had told her that a really long time ago women and children would stand out there to watch and wait for the return of the whaling ships in the harbor. Those ships held their husbands and fathers, and sometimes they never returned because the voyages were so long and dangerous back then. Lauren got the chills just thinking about it. She hesitated to tell Chrissy about it though. She also wanted to show Chrissy the whaling museum, and best of all, the town's wonderful old library, but she decided not to do that today. What if Chrissy thought that stuff was boring or dorky? Maybe she'd just see what Chrissy liked and go along with that.

Main Street was busy, full of slow-moving cars and bicycles, the wide sidewalks crowded with people milling along. Officially dressed village traffic officers, most of them college kids on break for the summer, directed traffic, gave directions, and politely asked idling drivers to move on.

Lauren pointed places out as they made their way toward the end of the street, where they could see fancy sailing boats docked at the pier. "That's a really good book store," said Lauren. "And this is a fun place to get cool jewelry and funky hair stuff, and that store across the street has awesome clothes that aren't too expensive."

"I love all the outside restaurants," said Chrissy, marveling.

"Yeah, we'll probably go to a few of them. Oh, and there. That's Rudy's, the ice cream place I told you about. The place where I had the Conversation." They stopped and peered inside. The place was packed with customers.

"Let's walk all the way down, okay?" asked Lauren, as she gestured down the street toward the ocean.

It was a short walk to the end of Main Street, and then a right turn, which took them past the harbor, parallel to the ocean. About a quarter of a mile down the narrow lane lined with tall sea grasses, Lauren turned left onto a sandy pathway, which quickly changed to a weather-beaten boardwalk. Three steps up, and they emerged on the beach.

Chrissy gasped. "Wow! It's amazing." She stood and stared, the wind whipping her hair around her face.

Lauren was secretly thrilled at Chrissy's enthusiasm because she had a hard time taking charge. "You need to assert yourself!" her dad often told her. Easier said than done. She didn't like to stick out. It was always just easier to go with the flow or stay in the background. If Olivia wanted to go to the mall, or Padma suggested ice-skating, or Jessica wanted to go see a movie, Lauren always just agreed. She always ended up having a good time. The beach was her special place, though, and she really wanted Chrissy to think it was special too.

The beach was wide and long, with soft, white, sand and rolling waves that swelled and broke, gently lapping the wide shoreline. Despite the fact that it was late in the afternoon, there were still quite a few people lounging there, mostly teenagers, and a few families with small kids. Down the beach, Lauren could see a group of boys playing Frisbee.

"This is where I usually hang out," said Lauren. "I like to—" She froze and clutched Chrissy's arm.

"Lauren! What is it!" said Chrissy, alarmed. "Do you have a stomachache?" Then Chrissy followed Lauren's gaze. Lauren was staring at the boys playing Frisbee.

Lauren could barely speak. "It's him," she whispered. "Don't look. Don't look. Okay, now! Look! Do you see him? Wait, turn, turn. Did he see us?"

"Which one is he?" asked Chrissy, trying to look out of the corner of her eye.

"He has a red bathing suit on. The tall one with the shaggy blond hair. Why didn't I brush my hair before we left? Does this T-shirt look okay?" Lauren could feel her heart thumping in her chest like a big bass drum. She darted another look. He must have grown six inches since last summer. She wouldn't have thought it possible, but Charlie had gotten even better looking over the past year!

"You look gorgeous," said Chrissy loyally. "Your hair is all wind-swept but looks perfect, like a model.

And that T-shirt is super cute." She looked down the beach again. "He is definitely a hottie," she confirmed. "Who are the other guys?"

"I think his best friend is Frank something-or-other," said Lauren, trying to pull herself together and not sound so out of breath. "I forget the other ones, but I've seen a few of them over the past couple of summers. I'm pretty sure at least two are cousins of Charlie's. Do you have any lip gloss?"

Chrissy dug through her small canvas purse but came up empty handed. "Let's walk," she suggested, pulling Lauren onto the sand and turning in the direction of the boys.

Lauren's eyes widened. "We can't! We can't just walk right past them! Can we?" This was definitely not part of the Plan.

"Sure, why not?" said Chrissy encouragingly. "We can pretend we're collecting shells."

"Oh, okay," said Lauren weakly. "But this was so not a part of the Plan! I have it all figured out. On a card back at the house. It's a flowchart." As soon as she'd said it, she realized how dumb it must sound to Chrissy, but Chrissy seemed unfazed by Lauren's fussing.

"We'll be spontaneous," laughed Chrissy. "Come on. I see a pretty shell."

She picked it up and showed it to Lauren. Lauren panicked. Chrissy was not understanding the importance of the Plan. If they didn't follow the Plan it would all be chaos . . . and then what? But, still. It was a walk on the beach. And Chrissy really wanted to go . . .

"Okay," agreed Lauren. "I'll act natural. I can do this. I just took a quiz about it, and I'm totally great at acting natural."

"A quiz?"

"Yep. In *Chic Chick* magazine. 'What's Your Flirting Style?' I didn't know if I was a Super Flirt, Just Fun, or Totally Chill. I am so totally awkward when I'm around guys, I figured I should find that out. Turns out, I'm Totally Chill, and a master at acting natural. So that's how I will act."

"Oh please," Chrissy said, rolling her eyes good naturedly. "Just act like yourself! My sister always tells me to act like myself around boys. She's had a lot of really cute boyfriends, so she totally knows what she's talking about."

Lauren gave a laugh. "Yeah, right. Myself. As if. Come on. Let's walk."

The two of them took off their flip-flops and walked along the smooth, shiny sand, their bare feet making perfect impressions as they walked. Their footprints quickly filled with swirling, foamy surf that roiled around the soles of their feet, tickling them.

As they moved past the boys, Lauren didn't know where to look. Her heart was beating so hard that she thought it would jump out of her chest. Or that Chrissy would hear it.

She started getting hot. Should she act like she didn't know they were there? Look up? Keep looking down and pretending to search for shells? Where was the plan for how to walk past your Huge Crush? That was it, there was no plan. She almost ran back the way they came. Without a plan, she didn't know what to do.

She was looking down, so she should have seen the hole in the sand, but she tripped anyway. *Oh great,* she thought. *Way to go.*

"Ooops!" said Chrissy, holding out an arm to steady her.

Lauren glanced over at the boys. They were probably totally laughing at her. But no one was even looking in their direction. They were way too immersed in their game of Frisbee, which was clearly more than just a game of toss-and-catch. It seemed to have elaborate rules, defenders, team play. She'd been studying how to play in the book she'd ordered, since she knew Charlie loved Frisbee, but because she was so nervous, she couldn't remember a single thing about it. What if the Frisbee landed right at her feet and she had to toss it back and it went backward into the ocean or something? She prayed it wouldn't land in front of her. But also secretly kind of hoped it would.

They kept walking and passed by. Lauren glanced at Chrissy, who met her gaze and shrugged. "Guess they were really into their game," Chrissy said.

"He doesn't even know I'm alive," moaned Lauren softly. "He didn't even say hi to me. Didn't so much as look at me."

Chrissy patted her friend on the shoulder. "Don't worry. We'll fix that. We'll—"

"Hey! Wait up!" called a male voice behind them.

chapter 4

LAUREN FROZE. CHARLIE. CHARLIE ANDERSON WAS
calling after her. She and Chrissy stopped. Then slowly,
oh-so-casually—or at least she hoped, since she read in
Chic Chick that acting casual was best—Lauren turned
around toward Charlie.

But it wasn't Charlie. It was that other guy, Charlie's
friend.

Frank.

"Hey, what's up?" called Chrissy.

Lauren wished she could be as natural as Chrissy, who
seemed to be a true master at acting casual. Lauren felt
so disappointed that she could barely keep her expression
normal.

Frank had trotted up the beach in their direction. He
was actually pretty cute, too. Not anywhere close to being
in Charlie's bracket, but cute in a skinny, dark-haired,

dark-eyed kind of way. His hair was kind of shaggy like Charlie's, though his was more curly and definitely wasn't sun-bleached like Charlie's. His bathing suit was all wrong, though. It was a faded blue, and so long it practically billowed around his knobby knees. Probably a hand-me-down from an older brother, Lauren decided.

"Do either of you guys have a Band-Aid?" he asked. "My friend just stepped on a sharp shell or something and cut his toe."

Lauren looked past Frank and drew in a quick breath. The other boys had stopped playing and were huddled around Charlie, who was standing on one leg like an adorable flamingo, one foot raised in the air, his hands on the shoulders of two of the other guys for balance. Charlie was hurt!

"I think I've got one," said Chrissy, rummaging around again through her small purse. She pulled out a rumpled Band-Aid and held it up triumphantly. "Here you go!"

How could Chrissy remain so calm under these circumstances? "Is Char—is your friend hurt badly?" Lauren stammered.

"Nah, he's fine," said Frank. "Just a little cut. But we want to get on with the game. My team is totally creaming them."

"Here, we'll help," said Chrissy, giving Lauren a look that said *pull yourself together and start participating!*

So Lauren pulled herself together and followed Chrissy right into the midst of the group of boys. She hoped she wouldn't suddenly, spontaneously trip again and fall flat on her face or something.

"I'm Frank," said Frank as they reached Charlie and his friends. "This is Charlie, Owen, Cody, Grant, Matt B. and Matt M."

Chrissy looked to Lauren to say something, but Lauren remained silent. Frozen. She couldn't say a word. Silently she blamed Chrissy. If they had followed the Plan she would have known exactly what to do and say.

"I'm Chrissy, and this is Lauren," Chrissy said, smiling encouragingly at Lauren and giving her another Look.

Chrissy was so natural, so calm. Lauren could barely look at the boys, let alone talk so easily to them.

"Show Chrissy your toe, Charlie," directed Frank. "She has a Band-Aid for you."

Charlie raised his foot higher and grinned that heartbreaking, sideways grin that Lauren loved so much. But he was grinning at Chrissy, not her. Why couldn't she have thought to carry Band-Aids with her?

"Let me prop my foot on you, Barnes," Charlie said to Matt B. Obligingly, Matt knelt down and allowed Charlie to prop his foot on Matt's knee for Chrissy's inspection.

Chrissy glanced at Lauren, silently asking, *What should I do?*, and then after an awkward moment, stooped down and examined Charlie's toe. Lauren could see a bit of red on it—it was bleeding slightly. She watched as Chrissy pulled a tissue from her bag and began dusting the sand from Charlie's foot, gently dabbing at the tiny cut. How Lauren wished she'd had a Band-Aid on her! How she wished those were her hands, gently brushing the sand from his wound.

"Ow! Not so hard!" howled Charlie.

Lauren giggled, then clamped a hand to her mouth. She couldn't have Charlie thinking she was laughing at him, though it was kind of funny that he was making such a big deal out of such a tiny cut. She always seemed to giggle at the worst times.

"Hold still," said Chrissy bossily, slapping him play-fully on the shin as she peeled the paper from the Band-Aid and applied it carefully to Charlie's toe. "I think you're going to live. There. Done."

"Thanks," said Charlie, unpropping his foot from Matt. B.'s knee.

"Nice to meet you guys," said Frank, as Owen picked up the Frisbee and made a motion to get the game going again.

Lauren knew she had to say something. "Nice to meet you, too!" she said, too quickly. "Well . . . see you around!" Why did she have to be so awkward around these guys? See you around? That was brilliant conversation.

"See you on the beach!" Chrissy said, and waved good-bye with a smile.

Lauren and Chrissy turned and headed away in the direction they'd come. There was another path leading off the beach just a short way down.

As soon as they were far enough away from the boys to be out of earshot, Lauren let out a long, breathy sigh. "Isn't he gorgeous, Chrissy? Did you see how awesome he was?"

"Yeah, he's definitely good looking," agreed Chrissy.

"No, really. Is he not the cutest guy on the Eastern Seaboard?"

"Yes. Yes, he is," said Chrissy patiently. "I'll grant you that, since Justin is on the West Coast! I was trying to figure out a way to give you the Band-Aid, so you could put it on him, but it seemed too awkward."

"Yeah, well, thanks for thinking about that. What about his friends? Did you think any of them were cute? Like Frank? He's pretty cute, right? Kind of skinny, but whatever. Or what's his name, one of the Matts? Wouldn't it be amazing if you started going out with one of Charlie's friends and we could, like, go out on double dates?"

"Yeah, no. I doubt it," said Chrissy, shaking her head. "Justin, remember? My adorable crush from back home?"

"Right!" said Lauren. "I know." Then she thought about it. "It would just be good if you liked one of the boys so we could be together, like a foursome. Plus Frank is kind of cute."

"I guess Frank kind of looks like Justin," Chrissy said finally. "If you squint a little."

"Perfect! Just think. You could switch your crush to Frank, just for the next few weeks. We could play beach volleyball together, couples-style. We could hang out at the snack bar—this beach has an awesome snack bar, but it's back the other direction so I'll show you tomorrow— and we could maybe go for ice cream at Rudy's, and there's this way-fun Fourth of July barbecue at the Beach

Club that the whole town is invited to and we could go together, the four of us!"

Chrissy laughed and gently cut Lauren off. "Okay, I promise to think about it. In support of your plan. And in support of you. But like I said, my heart belongs to Justin! You should know what that's like. It would be like me asking you to stop having a crush on Charlie."

"Never!" Lauren cried.

"See?" said Chrissy laughing.

Still, Lauren was happy that Chrissy promised to think about it. She thought about the Fourth of July barbecue and how much fun all four of them would have, and sighed happily. "I just can't help it. I took a quiz in my magazine—it says I'm a 'hopeless romantic.'"

Chrissy laughed again and shook her head. "That sounds about right."

Lauren linked her arm in Chrissy's as they headed up the wooden boardwalk and exited the beach. "This is going to be an awesome vacation," she said. "I can just tell. Tomorrow, we can initiate Operation Cell Phone." And then Lauren added silently to herself *and Operation Get Chrissy to Forget Justin and Fall for Frank!*

"SO I'VE BEEN DOING SOME STUDYING," SAID LAUREN
the next morning as the girls packed their beach bags up
in Lauren's room.

"Studying?" asked Chrissy, bewildered. "Did you
tackle that math packet already?"

"Not for school," laughed Lauren. "Studying up on
sports. I've been reading the sports section of the paper
practically every day since last summer. And I have a
how-to book on Frisbee, so I now know how to throw,
sort of. I have determined that Charlie has to be either a
Mets or a Yankees fan, because he's from New York, so
I studied both teams. See, the Mets are in the National
League, and the Yankees are in the American League,
so it's a fifty-fifty shot which team he roots for. And also
I found this on my parents' book shelf." She held up a
thick book for Chrissy to see.

"*Moby-Dick*?" asked Chrissy, puzzled.

"Yep. Last summer I saw Charlie reading some really big book at the beach. So I know he's an intellectual. I figured this would impress him."

Chrissy stopped rolling up her towel and looked at Lauren. "Why do you need to pretend? I mean, you're already smart. And you love baseball. But I happen to know you're a hardcore Yankees fan. And don't you love reading mysteries? What's wrong with that?"

"Fun mystery books don't send the same message as nineteenth-century novels," Lauren explained patiently. "And I like baseball but I don't know a lot about any other sports. And guys talk sports with one another. Talking about sports will be my icebreaker. You totally need to have one of those. Charlie will be impressed by my knowledge of baseball and Frisbee and it will give us something to talk about."

"Oh . . . kay," said Chrissy, drawing the word out slowly.

"Do you want to see my flowchart?"

"Oh yeah, your flowchart," said Chrissy. "You mentioned something about that before."

Lauren pulled the card out from under a pile of magazines on the bedside table and showed it to Chrissy. "It's my plan. My plan to start a real conversation with him, plus give him my number at the same time. It's foolproof. I've got every possible angle covered."

Chrissy glanced down at it. Her eyes flickered over the card as she read it. She smiled and handed it back to Lauren, but didn't say anything.

It was a bright, sunny day, warm but not sweltering— perfect beach weather. They walked through town and headed toward Crane's Beach, where they'd seen the boys the previous afternoon.

It was much more crowded, but Lauren spotted Charlie almost at once. It was as though her eyes were drawn to him by an unseen power. He was with his friends again, but this time they were playing what appeared to be an intense game of badminton. Today he wore black swim trunks instead of the red ones he'd had on yesterday. Was he still wearing Chrissy's Band-Aid? She couldn't see, but she secretly hoped he had changed it and was wearing a new one.

"There they are," said Lauren to Chrissy, gesturing with a quick jerk of her chin.

Chrissy turned to see the boys, just as Charlie laid out horizontally, the arm with the racket stretched to its limit, and thwacked the birdie back over the net before landing face down in the sand.

"Oof," said Chrissy, wincing, as she and Lauren watched Charlie pick himself up and dust the sand from his front. "That just didn't seem worth it."

"He's really into sports," said Lauren, shaking her head admiringly. "Come on. Let's pretend we haven't seen them and spread our blanket near theirs. I think I know which towels are theirs. I made a note of them from last summer."

There was a good space on the far side of the boys' towels, closer to the water, and the girls spread out their blanket, studiously avoiding looking in the boys' direction.

"Has he seen us?" asked Lauren through the side of her mouth.

"I don't think so," said Chrissy.

"Well, guess I'll get some reading done, then," said Lauren with a sigh. She settled back on her side of the blanket, propped her head against her tote bag, and opened up *Moby-Dick*.

"How is it?" asked Chrissy a few minutes later, turning a page of her paperback.

Lauren shifted uncomfortably. The truth was, she'd read the same line over and over again and was having a hard time focusing. "It's okay. But the book is so heavy,

I can't really hold it up to read for very long without my arms starting to ache . . ." She was dying to start the novel she packed. Her English teacher had recommended it and it seemed so good. But, she reminded herself, she needed to stay on plan. On the Plan. And the Plan called for *Moby-Dick*.

"Psst! They're coming!" hissed Chrissy.

Lauren's heart gave a wallop inside her chest. She clutched the book tighter and raised it up to her face, hoping Charlie would see the title and realize how smart she was. He'd probably already read it, and maybe he would want to discuss it with her over strawberry frappés next week.

Out of the corner of her eye (thank goodness for sunglasses, which made it easy to be discreet while spying), Lauren saw the boys arrive at their towels. "Are you ready for Operation Cell Phone?" Lauren whispered to Chrissy.

"Yes, sir," said Chrissy.

"Let's review," said Lauren. "What happens first?"

"You sit up. You reach casually into your bag. Then you start to freak out a little bit," said Chrissy. "You pull everything out of your bag. I sit up and start helping you look for whatever is missing. Then you oh-so-casually pretend you see the guys sitting near us. You walk over. You ask Charlie if he has a cell phone you can borrow to call yours, because you think it might be buried somewhere in all our stuff. The rest is . . . future history."

"Exactly," said Lauren. "Commence phase one now."

"Um, but there's one small problem," said Chrissy.

"What?"

"Looks like the guys are heading into the water for a swim."

Lauren darted a glance sideways. Chrissy was right! The guys were heading to the water. She groaned softly. "What is with boys these days?" she demanded. "Don't they ever sit still?" She pondered. She visualized her flowchart. What should she do now? Plan, she thought to herself. A plan was contingent on one thing happening, then another. They were swimming now. So what would happen after they swam? Then she had it.

"Let's go to the snack bar," said Lauren. "Chances are when they get out of the water they'll be thirsty."

"Good plan," agreed Chrissy.

The snack bar was small, with just six weather-beaten tables near it. But it served hot dogs, hamburgers, and fries, as well as a wide variety of drinks and ice-cream bars. There were six stools at the shady Formica counter, and two friendly, older teenage guys working behind it. Only two of the stools were taken, by a father and his tiny daughter, who was eating a drippy Popsicle. Chrissy and Lauren took the two middle seats, leaving empty ones on either side. They ordered lemonades.

"How long do you think we should wait for them?" asked Chrissy after they'd been sitting about ten minutes, drinking their lemonades very slowly. The father and daughter left, leaving them the only ones at the counter. Two families showed up, pulled two tables together, and sat down. Chrissy sighed and looked around.

"Five more minutes?" suggested Lauren. "They have to be thirsty after all that badminton, right? I mean—" She stopped, swiveling back around to face the counter. "They're coming!" she hissed. "Quick! Start talking sports!"

"Sports?" Chrissy hissed back. "I don't know anything about—"

"So, how 'bout that off-season trade by the Knicks, huh?" said Lauren loudly. She felt someone approach the counter on her other side. "Why would they ever give up such a quality point guard for a mediocre small forward?"

"Hey!" said a boy's voice at Lauren's left elbow. She jumped. And turned.

It was Frank.

"I disagree. He's a shoot-first point guard, and that's not what we need right now," said Frank.

"What?" said Lauren. Was he talking to her? Oh! Oh no! He was talking sports back to her! Where was Charlie? Had he even heard what she'd said? "Oh," she said, flustered. "Um . . . yeah, well, that's debatable."

"You're Frank, right?" said Chrissy, smoothly interrupting the awkward moment. Lauren had never felt more grateful to someone in her entire life.

"Yep, I'm Frank," said Frank. He seemed pleased to be remembered. "Frank Fowler."

Lauren realized that Charlie was now on Chrissy's other side. She heard Charlie order two hot dogs and a lemonade. He liked lemonade . . . something else they had in common! Frank ordered large fries and a soda. Lauren felt Chrissy nudge her leg under the counter, and knew she had to say something.

"So," she said, addressing Charlie, turning her back a little to Frank. "I'm reading *Moby-Dick*. It's . . . it's awesome. It's . . . about this whale." As soon as the words were out of her mouth she regretted them. Stupid! What a stupid conversation opener! She should have talked sports, but that dumb Frank had thrown her off by responding to her icebreaker. Oh the Plan . . . what was the Plan? The Plan was Operation Cell Phone. So why was she talking about sports already? She knew if she didn't follow the Plan it would be a mess . . .

Charlie leaned forward, past Chrissy, and gave Lauren a quizzical look, raising one eyebrow.

"*Moby-Dick*?" Frank repeated. "My older brother read that in college last year. That's pretty serious for beach reading, no?"

"Oh, well, yeah, but I—"

"Order up!" yelled one of the guys behind the counter. The other one slid Frank's fries and drink to him on Lauren's left, and the first one slid Charlie's hot dogs and lemonade to him on the other side of Chrissy.

"Well, see you guys," said Frank.

Charlie didn't say anything, but he followed Frank out of the snack area, cramming half a hot dog into his mouth as he walked.

Lauren groaned and slowly lowered her face down to the counter, where she rested her forehead on it. "Why did I have to talk about *Moby-Dick*?" she moaned.

Chrissy patted her back. "It's okay," she said. "But I think you should just be yourself from now on."

Lauren picked her head up and looked at Chrissy. "Myself? Why would an awesome, supersmart guy like Charlie want to hang out with me? I have to show him that there's more to me than meets the eye, and that we have a lot in common. Come on. Let's go try Operation Cell Phone before they go back into the water or start playing some new sport." She thought she heard Chrissy sigh again. "What?" she asked.

"Nothing," said Chrissy.

When they got back to their stuff, Lauren walked Chrissy through the plan one more time. "So then I go over there, and I tell them I've lost my phone and ask Charlie if he would mind coming over here to call it. And then I make a flirtatious comment about how now he has my number, and maybe he should call me sometime. Got it?"

"Got it," said Chrissy. "But you'd better hurry, because they look like they're getting ready to get up again and go swimming or something."

Lauren scrambled to her feet, readjusting her bathing suit and shaking out her hair so it was just right. "Okay, here goes," she said firmly, and turned and marched toward the boys.

"Wait, Laur!" called Chrissy.

But Lauren was almost at the boys' towels. Too late to turn back now. She figured Chrissy was going to give her another pep talk about how she should be herself and not try to talk about topics she knew nothing about. Whatever.

She cleared her throat. "Um, hi, guys," she said, stopping and looking down at them. The boys had been passing around a bottle of sunblock. Charlie looked up, shielding his eyes from the sun to see her.

"Hey. Karen, right?"

"Um, close. Lauren." She gulped, trying to steady herself. He had almost remembered her name! Do. Not. Screw. This. Up. "So I have a favor to ask you," she said, waving her hand. Then she froze, horrified.

She was holding her cell phone in her hand. She'd forgotten to "hide" it before walking over here. That must have been what Chrissy had wanted to say to her. Why hadn't Chrissy tried harder to get her attention! Now what was she going to say? She couldn't exactly ask them to help her find her lost cell phone when there it was in her hand!

"What's up?" asked Charlie.

Think fast. Think fast. "Um, I was wondering if one of you might have . . . might have . . ." Think. Think. Aha! "—might have a portable radio I could borrow? To check the score of the Yankee game?"

"No, sorry," said Charlie. "But why don't you just check on your phone? Don't you have internet?"

"Oh, well no, but whatever . . ." said Lauren quickly, turning away before Charlie could see that her face had turned bright red.

"Hey!" Frank called after her.

She stopped.

"Just so you know, the Yanks aren't playing this afternoon. The Mets have a double header, though."

"Oh, right," said Lauren with a queasy giggle. "My bad. Well, I guess I'll have to tune in tomorrow." She hurried back to Chrissy and flopped down next to her, wishing that the sand would somehow turn into quicksand and swallow her.

"Guess it didn't go so well?" Chrissy asked with a sympathetic look on her face.

"You have no idea," Lauren replied. "It's my plan. It's the *perfect* plan. So how come I keep messing it up?"

THE NEXT SEVERAL DAYS WERE OVERCAST AND
rainy. The girls entertained themselves by jogging together
in the warm rain, shopping at stores on Main Street, going
to the small local movie theater, and even cooking dinner
for Lauren's parents one night. They went shopping with
Mrs. Silver for corn and tomatoes at the local farm stand,
for fresh fish at the local fish store, and for crusty bread
at the local bakery. Then they grilled scallops (with a little
help from Mr. Silver, master griller), made corn on the
cob, and tomato and mozzarella salad. It was fun having
someone to hang out with. Normally Lauren would just
hang out by herself or spend time with Mom and Dad, but
it was great to have company. Being an only child meant
she could entertain herself pretty well, but having Chrissy
around was like having a twenty-four-hour pal.

Lauren and Chrissy spent one morning at the library,

where Lauren showed Chrissy her favorite reading nooks. Lauren realized, as they talked about books, that they both loved a few of the same authors. Lauren looked longingly over at the paperback mysteries that seemed to be calling her name . . . but she was determined to get through *Moby-Dick* by the July Fourth picnic so she could talk about it with Charlie. So far she had read eighteen pages. Chrissy borrowed Lauren's library card and checked out a paperback from a series Lauren recommended. Lauren looked around hoping to see Charlie. "At the library?" asked Chrissy. "Somehow I doubt it." Lauren wondered what Chrissy meant, but decided not to say anything.

Finally, after what seemed like forever, the sun came out. Lauren suggested they get to the beach early so that they could be there before the guys and not look as though they were stalkers.

"But we'll do our stakeout near where we were last time," said Lauren matter-of-factly as they walked to the beach, laden down with tote bags full of towels, a blanket, water, sunblock, and of course, books. "Because people are creatures of habit."

"What do you mean by that?" asked Chrissy.

"Well, I bet you and your family always sit in the same

seats at your dinner table, right? And at school? Don't you always sit in the same seat? So chances are, they'll park their towels in the same area they did last time we were at the beach together."

"Good point," said Chrissy. "Maybe you should be a detective. Or a social anthropologist."

"What's that?" asked Lauren.

"My sister wants to study social anthropology when she starts college in a few years. It's a science that studies how groups of people behave. Liz is already really into it. That's why she gives such great advice about boys and dating and stuff—she knows a lot about why people act the way they do."

Lauren couldn't help but wonder what it would be like to have an older sister. When she was little, she used to beg her parents to have another child so she could be the big sister, but they never did. Then as she got older she changed her mind and decided it was actually nice being an only child. She didn't have to share her clothes or books or makeup with anyone. But then again, having an older sister to borrow those things from was probably fun. And having an older sister who knew a lot could come in handy. An older sister might be able to help with the Love Plan.

The girls climbed the stairs to the beach. It was still early, not yet ten, so not many people were there. They headed toward their spot.

"I'm sure Charlie has heard of social anthropology," said Lauren, pulling out the blanket and handing one side to Chrissy so they could spread it out. "He's probably the top student in his class. He probably read *Moby-Dick* when he was in preschool." They both plunked down on the blanket.

"Well, why don't you ask him?" suggested Chrissy. "Because he's heading this way!"

Lauren stared at Chrissy in a panic. "How do I look?" she asked desperately.

"Awesome. But you'd look even more awesome if you didn't look totally panicked! Just relax."

"Right. Must relax. Look casual," said Lauren. She pulled off her T-shirt and adjusted her suit. Then she settled back against her tote bag, which she was using to prop her head up, and readjusted her sunglasses. "I can't look. You need to be my eyes. Is he with the same group of guys as last time? Frank and all those guys?"

Chrissy pretended to do a stretch, twisting her torso this way and that, so she could scope Charlie out. "No," she said. "He's with his mom and dad. And maybe his grandmother? And a couple of older guys and one older girl—I'm guessing they're his cousins?"

"The guys are his cousins," confirmed Lauren. She didn't even need to look—she knew everything about his family. "The girl is his older sister. And that would be his grandmother. He's so nice and respectful to her. He's totally like, the perfect guy. I read in my magazine that it's important to find a guy who is close to his family and respectful of elders. Here, let me put sunblock on you so I can get an angle."

"Well, I already sunblocked," said Chrissy, but then Lauren gave her a look that said *pretty please,* so she turned to face Charlie's family so that Lauren could sit behind her and scope them out while she applied sunblock to Chrissy's back.

Lauren stole a look at Charlie and his family as they settled themselves in to their spot. It was not far away, maybe twenty yards or so. No one was yet camped in between them. Charlie sat down to rummage through a tote bag, and then spotted the girls. He smiled ever so slightly, and jerked his chin up quickly in a gesture of greeting.

"He said hello!" squeaked Lauren under her breath. "I can't look. You look." She flopped back down onto the blanket next to Chrissy. "What's he doing now?"

"He's getting out his book," Chrissy reported. "It's a thick one. It looks like a history book of some sort."

"See, I told you he was smart. He reads all the time when he's with his family. I bet they are a really academic family," said Lauren. "Well, I can't exactly do Operation Cell Phone if he's with his family. I'll focus on making him think I'm a reader like he is."

"But you *are* a reader," said Chrissy. "All year long you seemed to have a different book with you every week. And you must have a hundred books in your bedroom. Plus, you practically knew where everything in the town library was by heart. You don't have to pretend to be a reader, Laur!"

Lauren sat up and scrambled through her bag. She hauled out *Moby-Dick*. "You know what I mean. He reads way more important books than I do," she pointed out. "Didn't you say he was reading some thick history book? I need to impress him, and a regular old paperback is not going to cut it!" She opened her book to a random page in the middle and pretended to become engrossed in reading it, holding it in such a way that Charlie would be able to see the title, which wasn't easy given how thick the book was.

Half an hour went by.

Lauren's eyes grew droopy. Her arms ached from holding up the book, which she'd gradually lowered until it sat propped on her stomach. The warm sunlight seemed to glare brighter, the white of the page blinding her despite her sunglasses. The lulling, rhythmic whoosh of the surf, the caw of the seagulls overhead, the happy shouts of young children building a sandcastle . . . all worked together to make her very sleepy . . .

Then Chrissy nudged her. "His friends just showed up! He's putting away his book and standing up to join them. He's saying good-bye to his parents. Looks like the parents and the cousins are packing up to go."

Lauren was suddenly wide awake. She rolled over onto her stomach, pretending to continue reading, but she was able to check out what was going on with Charlie. It was just as Chrissy had described it. His parents, grandmother, sister, and older cousins were trudging back toward the stairs leading away from the beach. Charlie stood with his back to the girls, talking with his friends. Lauren was able to check out his back and see that he had some seriously nice back muscles, all brown and shiny with sunblock. He looked especially good standing next to his friends, who were still skinny boys. She could stare at his back all day.

Then Charlie turned and looked in their direction. Had he caught Lauren checking him out? She crossed her fingers that her sunglasses camouflaged her gawking stare. He did that chin-up-hello thing, and once again smiled a little, that half-grin. He was smiling at them! At her! Was this really happening? Was he—wait! Was he actually walking over to talk to them? Frank was with him, but Lauren had eyes only for Charlie. Her heart started to race again and she felt her hands get all sweaty. As the boys neared the girls, Lauren squeezed her eyes shut behind her dark glasses, willing herself not to squeal out loud.

"Hey," said Charlie, staring down at them, casting a shadow across both girls.

"Hey," replied Lauren and Chrissy at the same time.

Frank spoke up. "We're heading to the snack bar. You guys want to come grab something to eat with us?"

"Sure," said both girls at the same time again.

The four of them joined up with the four other guys. Lauren recognized both the Matts, Owen, and—was his name Grant?—she couldn't remember. Who cared? She was walking to the snack bar right next to Charlie!

The Matts were gabbing away behind them, talking about some new skateboard park that was opening up close to the beach.

Lauren could feel Charlie walking alongside her. She caught a whiff of his coconut-scented sunblock. She looked down at his large feet trudging through the hot sand next to her smaller ones. Walking side by side together looked so—couple-like. He was so tall! She thought about how deliriously amazing it would be to have his broad shoulder to rest her cheek on during a slow dance. Could he tell what she was thinking just by looking at her? But he wasn't looking at her. His gaze was fixed straight ahead. Lauren decided he must be lost in deep thoughts. Maybe he was contemplating beach erosion or the plight of the endangered sea turtle. Lauren tried to remember everything she could about endangered sea turtles. Did they even live this far north? If they didn't, would she sound totally clueless bringing them up? At the exact moment she drew up the nerve to say something, Charlie turned around to say something to one of the Matts, something about skateboarding that she couldn't hear. But as he turned, his arm brushed against her shoulder. An electric shock rippled through her entire body. Had he done it on purpose? She had no way of knowing for sure.

At the snack bar, she and Chrissy ordered french fries to share, and lemonades. The boys ordered full-blown meals, even though it wasn't yet eleven. Lauren noted with satisfaction that Charlie ordered lemonade again too.

"You have to talk to him!" Chrissy hissed in Lauren's ear, as they moved to a table to sit. The boys, having ordered a lot more food, remained standing at the counter, still waiting for their orders.

"What should I talk about?" asked Lauren. "The Plan just covers getting my phone number to him. It didn't cover actually talking. And I get so totally tongue-tied when he's next to me."

"Didn't you say he was a big nature lover?" said Chrissy.

"Yes! Maybe when we walk back to the beach, I'll bring up marine ecosystems or something. I reread that chapter in my bio book before I left for vacation, so I should be able to sound intelligent."

"Why don't you just talk about how his summer is going?" suggested Chrissy.

Lauren looked horrified. "That's so boring!" she said.

There wasn't room at the table for all of them, so the

other four boys sat together at a table next to theirs. Charlie and Frank joined Chrissy and Lauren. Charlie wasn't very talkative, and Lauren felt as though she had basically lost the ability to speak, so she didn't say much. Frank and Chrissy carried most of the conversation, chatting about everything from movies to TV shows to favorite bands. Both Frank and Chrissy tried to pull Lauren into the conversation a few times, but Lauren remained quiet. Charlie obviously thought the conversation wasn't academic enough, so she would remain quiet and mysterious, just like him. Frank was talking about how much he loved baseball and even though Lauren did too she felt that she shouldn't talk with Frank if Charlie wasn't joining in.

After they'd eaten, the group walked back toward the beach. In front of her, Lauren watched Charlie fall into step next to Chrissy. Chrissy glanced behind her at Lauren and gave a little apologetic shrug.

Lauren found herself walking next to Frank. She barely heard a word he was saying. Something about where he was from, and then about some party his parents were making him go to. She kind of wished he would shut up so she could hear what Charlie was saying to Chrissy.

Chrissy stooped down, pretending to fix the strap

on her flip-flop. She and Lauren exchanged quick looks. Lauren nodded gratefully and quickened her pace so that she was soon walking alongside Charlie.

They proceeded in silence. Then Lauren pointed over toward the dunes. "So, I was studying up a little on the shoreline ecosystem around here," she said. "I didn't know that eelgrass provides essential habitat to fish and foraging birds."

"Um . . . huh," said Charlie, glancing around behind him. "That's cool," he said. "Yo, Fowler. Do I get a rematch? This time prepare to be crushed in v-ball, man."

"In your dreams, Anderson," replied Frank, who was walking behind Lauren.

"See you, guys," said Charlie to Lauren and Chrissy. He and Frank grabbed a ball and headed toward the net, which was open.

Chrissy and Lauren flopped down next to each other on their blanket.

"I tried to talk about ecosystems, but obviously he knew so much more about it than I do," moaned Lauren. "I sounded like such an idiot. Plan B fail."

chapter 7

"IT'S NOT GOING TO BE A LATE EVENING," SAID Lauren's dad, peering in the rearview at Lauren and Chrissy. "I'm sure the food will be fantastic. The Claussens don't skimp when it comes to catering parties."

"And maybe there will even be some kids your age!" added Lauren's mom brightly. She pulled down the flap to look in the mirror as she applied some lipstick.

"There are never kids our age at these things," muttered Lauren. She glanced up and saw her dad giving her a Look in the rearview mirror. "But don't worry, guys," she added hastily. "We'll be charming."

Lauren's dad pulled up behind a long line of cars that were parked along the road, outside a huge house overlooking the beach. It was a much larger party than Lauren had expected.

Lauren and Chrissy were dressed in T-shirts and

shorts and sandals, their hair still damp from showering, their faces pink from a day at the beach, despite the gobs of sunblock they'd applied.

"Why don't you go around to the back of the house, where the pool is?" suggested Lauren's dad. "I'm sure that's where the kids will be congregating."

"It's so cool that your parents didn't make us get all dressed up," said Chrissy as the girls walked around to the backyard. "My parents totally make me dress up every time we go someplace with lots of grown-ups."

"This party wasn't really worth assembling an outfit," replied Lauren. "I mean, it's bound to be a bunch of three-year-olds. And anyway, as far as personal style this summer, shorts and tees are now my go-to clothing. Charlie's got a really laid back style, and now so do I."

Chrissy shook her head. "What's wrong with just being yourself, Laur? It's like my sister, Liz, always says— if you have to change your whole personality and your style to get a guy to like you, well, maybe he's not the right guy."

Lauren didn't answer. But she was kind of annoyed by Chrissy's question, and she was getting a little tired of hearing about Chrissy's sister's supposedly wonderful advice. What did Liz know anyway? Lauren had always liked wearing shorts and tees. Sure, in the past she would have put a little more effort into her outfit for a party, but now she realized that having a supercasual personal style, like Charlie, was actually really cool. And now that she really thought about it, what did Chrissy know about it? Well, so okay, she was kind of, sort of, seeing Justin, so Lauren supposed Chrissy had more boyfriend experience than she did. But not *that* much more. Chrissy was good at talking to the boys on the beach, but it's not like she was good at flirting with them or anything. Besides, *Chic Chick* had an article all about matching your personal styles. Her style had to match Charlie's.

Chrissy touched Lauren's arm. "Looks like there are kids our age here."

A bunch of kids their age and a little older were crowded around a table full of food and drinks, talking and laughing. Lauren's heart skipped a beat. Was Charlie here?

A quick scan of the pool area told her he wasn't. But Frank Fowler was. Why was he always around instead of Charlie?

Lauren leaned in to whisper to Chrissy. "Why don't you go talk to Frank? I think he likes you. He's looking over here."

Chrissy made a scoffing noise. "He doesn't like me. And I told you. I like Justin. I'm not interested."

"I know, I know . . . Justin. But would you do it for me? For the Plan?"

Chrissy looked at Lauren and opened her mouth like she was going to say something, but didn't.

"Lauren!" said a voice behind them.

It was Mrs. Claussen, the hostess, standing next to Lauren's mom.

"Look at you! You've gotten so tall!" she said, hurrying up to Lauren and hugging her. Lauren was enveloped in a cloud of perfume. Mrs. Claussen's earrings and many bracelets made little tinkly sounds.

"Thanks," she said awkwardly. She really hadn't gotten that much taller. Why did adults always, always talk about how tall a kid had gotten? "This is my friend, Chrissy Porter."

"Hello, Chrissy!" said Mrs. Claussen. Suddenly she swooped down and caught a little kid who was running by, chasing another little kid. She held up the kicking child, who didn't seem to know he was airborne.

"This is Bobby! Remember Bobby, Lauren?"

"Gee, yeah, hey, Bobby," said Lauren to the wiggling toddler. "You've gotten so . . . big." Okay, whatever. He had grown bigger since she'd last seen him. He had chocolate around his mouth, but he was still pretty cute.

"Hi!" said Bobby grumpily, squirming to be put back down. Mrs. Claussen set him down again as though he were a large sticky wind-up toy, and he continued on his way, chasing a couple of kids around the back patio area, weaving in and around other partygoers.

"These girls look so mature," said Mrs. Claussen to Mrs. Silver. "It must be so nice to have older, more independent children! I love my boys, of course, but they are always going, going, going. What I wouldn't give for a couple hours of peace and quiet on the beach!"

Lauren could practically see the wheels turning in her mother's head.

"I have a great idea!" her mom said, her eyes dancing with excitement. "Why don't you let Lauren and Chrissy take the boys to the beach one day? They can be mother's helpers and play with the kids while you have a little relaxation time!"

Mrs. Claussen looked delighted. "Really?" she asked Mrs. Silver, who nodded, happy to be helping her friend. "What do you think, girls?" she asked Lauren and Chrissy.

The girls looked at each other and shrugged. Lauren didn't think a day at the beach with kids would interfere with the Plan. In fact, it might even help, given the fact that Charlie loved kids. "Sure thing," said Lauren. "No problem."

"How about Friday?" asked Mrs. Claussen. "I can go get my nails done for the first time in months. Would that be okay? I'll pay you, of course."

The girls nodded.

"We'll meet you at Crane's Beach at ten," said Mrs. Claussen delightedly. "Near the lifeguard stand?" She gave both the girls a big, jangly, perfumey hug and then hurried off with Lauren's mom by her side.

The girls watched Bobby whap another little kid over the head with a swimming pool noodle, then drop the noodle and race away.

"Is that Bobby's brother?" asked Chrissy.

"Mmm-hmm," said Lauren.

Both girls giggled. Lauren felt glad that their uncomfortable moment from earlier seemed to have passed.

"Are you sure you guys know what you're getting your-selves into?" asked a voice in Lauren's ear. She jumped. It was Frank. Yet again. Didn't he have anything to do other than show up all the time? And if he was going to do that, couldn't he at least make sure he had Charlie with him?

"I just heard Mrs. Claussen telling my mom you guys were going to be mother's helpers for her," said Frank, grinning. "Those kids are, um, shall we say, a tad boisterous?"

"You think?" laughed Chrissy as they watched Bobby's brother fire a supersoaking squirt gun at his brother's back, drenching him.

"Better you than me," said Frank, and slipped away again.

"You see?" said Lauren triumphantly. Her annoyance at Frank had quickly evaporated in her eagerness to get him together with Chrissy. "You two are perfect for each other! He's obviously smart. He just used the word 'bois-terous' in a sentence properly. And he's funny!"

Chrissy paused for a moment. She seemed unsure of what to say. Finally, she shrugged a little and said, "Well, he does remind me of Justin. But only a little bit! I'm still not switching my crush, Laur!"

Lauren's heart swelled. Chrissy had practically just admitted she thought Frank was cute. She could see it now. Double-dating with her best friend! Chrissy was her best friend now, right? And Charlie would be her boyfriend. It was turning into the perfect summer vacation.

chapter 8

"I HAD TOTALLY FORGOTTEN CRANE'S BEACH EVEN had a playground," said Lauren glumly. "I haven't been here since I was a little kid."

It was the following Friday. Another beautiful, perfect, sunny beach day, but Lauren and Chrissy were stuck at the playground, pushing Bobby and his brother, Kyle, on the swings. Lauren had done her best to convince the boys that they should go straight to the beach, but the boys were insistent about going to the playground first. Lauren knew that sometimes with kids this age, you just had to give in.

"I can see the guys from here," said Chrissy, peering through the tall sea grass on the dune in front of them.

"Me too," said Lauren gloomily. "To think I had Operation Cell Phone planned down to every possible angle, and I still haven't managed to execute it."

Below them and straight ahead, close to the water, were Charlie and four or five of his friends. They were playing some sort of running-around game with extremely intense rules that neither girl could follow.

"Higher!" squealed Bobby happily.

Lauren gave him a bigger push, then looked back and forth between Bobby and his brother, a thoughtful expression on her face.

"Uh-oh," said Chrissy. "I've seen that look before. You're cooking something up, aren't you?"

"I might be," said Lauren with a little smile playing on her lips. "Hey, Bobby," she said in a louder voice "How old are you?"

"Twee and a half!" he trilled.

"I'm four and three quarters!" chimed in Kyle.

"Wow," said Lauren. "You guys are big boys, aren't you?"

"I'm a big boy!" agreed Bobby. "Big, big boy!"

"I'm bigger!" yelled Kyle.

"You guys want to get a lemonade at the snack bar?" suggested Lauren.

"Yeahhhhhhhh!" shouted both boys together.

"You are totally bribing them!" said Chrissy.

Lauren shrugged. "All's fair in love and war, right? Besides, Mrs. Claussen said it was fine for them to have lemonade."

Chrissy laughed and rolled her eyes.

"Okay," said Lauren, catching Bobby by his chubby arms and skidding her feet forward until his swing stopped swinging. Chrissy did the same with Kyle.

"First we're going to play a fun game," said Lauren. "Then we'll go get lemonade."

Both boys bounced up and down excitedly in their swings.

"You see that big boy out there on the beach? The tall one with blond hair and a purple-and-white-striped bathing suit?"

"Yesp," said Bobby.

"You either say 'yes' or 'yep,'" Kyle explained to his brother.

"Yesp!" yelled Bobby.

"Okay, good," said Lauren, realizing it would be necessary to keep things moving along. "So here's what you guys do. We'll walk together down to the sand. We'll grab your buckets and shovels and stuff. We'll start building a sand castle. Then both of you can run up to that big boy and ask him, in your really cute and adorable way, to help us because we're going to build the world's biggest sand castle. And after we build it with him, you can ask him if he wants to come have lemonade with us. Can you remember all that?"

"Yesp!" yelled Bobby.

Kyle nodded excitedly.

"Okay! Race you guys to the buckets!"

A few minutes later, the boys and Chrissy and Lauren were happily digging in the sand.

"All right," said Lauren to Kyle. "Why don't you go ask that big boy now if he will come help us build the world's biggest sand castle?"

"First we gots to bury you, Lauren!" shouted Bobby.

"Yeahhhhh!" shouted Kyle.

Lauren sighed. "Fine. But then you go ask the big boy, okay?"

The boys were already digging a big hole for Lauren. It seemed to take forever, but finally it was long enough for her to settle into up to her waist with her legs out-stretched. The boys heaped mounds of sand over her, laughing delightedly.

Lauren let them pile on more and more sand, and then

told them that was enough. "Now go ask the big boy in the purple bathing suit to come help us make a castle, okay?"

The boys turned and raced toward Charlie and his friends, who'd moved a little farther away and were now involved in an intense game of Frisbee.

"I'll make myself scarce," said Chrissy, hopping up. "I'll take myself to the snack bar. I'll hang out there and wait for you guys. Sound good?"

"Sounds good," said Lauren, working her legs furiously to free herself from the packed, heavy sand. "See you soon."

Chrissy picked up her bag and headed off toward the snack bar. Lauren had just managed to extract herself from the hole and was frantically brushing away the sand from her legs when the little boys returned.

"We got the big boy to come help us build a castle!" shouted Kyle. "Just like you tolded us to!"

Lauren froze. Her back was still turned to them. She couldn't turn around. Was it possible to die of mortification? What would *Chic Chick* advise her to do? Damage control. She would play it oh-so-casual. "Aw, you guys, quit being so silly! I had no idea where you just went! Maybe the big boy doesn't want to help us. He looked pretty busy over there, playing with the other big boys."

"But, you tolded us—"

"That's okay," Charlie interrupted graciously. "I don't mind. Our Frisbee game just ended anyway. The rest of them are headed to the snack bar. And I'm a mad sand-castle builder."

The boys laughed with delight.

Lauren smiled and turned around.

But it wasn't Charlie she was giving what she hoped was her most dazzling smile.

It was Frank.

The plan had backfired. Again.

As Frank knelt down in the sand to help Bobby and Kyle begin building, Lauren spotted Chrissy far in the distance, turning onto the wooden boardwalk that led toward the snack bar. Just behind her were Charlie and his friends. Chrissy gave Lauren a helpless shrug, as though to say, *sorry, I tried*. Charlie was talking to Chrissy.

Just then, a thought struck Lauren. *It's not possible.* She tried to push it away. But the thought wouldn't go away. A tiny voice inside her asked: *What if Charlie likes Chrissy?*

chapter 9

A FEW DAYS LATER, ON MONDAY AFTERNOON, LAUREN
sat on the beach thinking. She hadn't seen Charlie at all
over the weekend. Had he gone home? Was his vacation
over so soon? That couldn't be. The previous summers
he'd been there when she arrived and remained there
when she'd left. She was almost positive his family spent
the whole summer in East Harbor. But where was he?
The Fourth of July barbecue was happening on Thursday.
He had to be there. She hadn't even had a chance to try
Operation Cell Phone on him!

Chrissy emerged from the water and joined Lauren
on the blanket, covering herself with a towel in an effort
to dry off.

"Just saw Matt B. in the water," she said, casually
wringing her hair and trying to comb it out with her fingers.

Lauren scrambled to a sitting position and stared at

her over the tops of her sunglasses. "And?" she prompted impatiently.

"And he told me that Charlie and his family have been in Montauk for the long weekend, visiting his cousins' family," she reported. "He's coming back later today."

Lauren let out a relieved sigh. "Thank goodness. I thought he wouldn't be here for the Fourth of July barbecue." Then a creeping suspicion entered her mind. "So, um, how did the subject come up? About Charlie, I mean? Did you ask Matt flat out, or did he volunteer the information?"

Chrissy shrugged and pulled out her book from her bag. "I asked," she said simply. "I thought you might want to know."

"Okay. Thanks," said Lauren. But her thoughts were whirling. What if Matt B. went and told Charlie that Chrissy had asked about him? Maybe Charlie would think it was Chrissy who wanted to know. Maybe Charlie would think Chrissy liked him. This wasn't good. And it most definitely was not part of the Plan.

The next morning Lauren awoke to the sound of rain pattering on the roof. She opened one eye and glanced at the clock. Already ten o'clock. In the next bed she could see that Chrissy was still sleeping, a mound underneath the bedspread that softly rose and fell, a pillow over her head. A tendril of auburn hair tumbled over the side of the bed. Lauren lay back on her own pillow and pondered.

Did Charlie really like Chrissy? Possibly. Did Chrissy like him back? She dismissed that possibility. Chrissy was still really hung up on her crush, Justin, back in California. She texted him every night and often during the day, too.

Plus Chrissy knew how crazy Lauren was about Charlie. She wouldn't do something like that. Would she? Not if she were really her BFF.

Quietly Lauren dug through her pile of magazines until she found the one she was looking for. She slid it off the bedside table and opened it carefully, so that the rattling of the page wouldn't awaken Chrissy. She turned to the quiz she remembered seeing there:

"Is your BFF really your Secret Frenemy?"

Back when Lauren had received this issue, she didn't have a BFF so there had been no reason to take the quiz. Plus, it didn't have anything to do with Charlie. But now,

Lauren thought, she had an almost BFF in Chrissy . . . at least she hoped she did . . . and maybe the quiz topic did have something to do with Charlie.

This is silly, she told herself. She stared at the quiz, unsure of what to do. But then she picked up the pen, determined to take the test for fun . . . just to see what it would tell her.

Can you trust your BFF with secrets?
(A) absolutely
(B) never
(C) not all of them—if it's a secret you're really worried might get around, you keep it to yourself

That was easy. The answer was A. Chrissy was totally trustworthy.

Does your BFF tell you things she doesn't tell anyone else?
(A) she tells me everything
(B) she tells me most things
(C) I don't know any of her secrets

Another easy one. A for sure. Chrissy had confided in Lauren about Justin. No one else at school knew about him. Telling about your secret crush pretty much qualified as telling everything.

> **There's a party coming up. You want to figure out if your secret crush will go with you. Your BFF:**
> **(A) asks him out on your behalf—without your permission**
> **(B) helps you figure out a plan to find out how he feels about you**
> **(C) asks him to go with her, even though she knows how you feel**

Another easy one: definitely *B*. Chrissy was always there to help her out when it came to Charlie. She thought about that for a minute. Maybe that was the solution! She should ask Chrissy to help her find out what Charlie thought about her! Once Charlie knew Lauren liked him, maybe he'd ask her to the Fourth of July party. The plan was a good one, Lauren was sure of it. She put down the magazine.

"Hey," said a sleepy voice in the next bed. Chrissy was awake and had lifted her head out from under the pillow. Her hair was a mass of glossy strands falling around her shoulders. Lauren wished her own hair would do that instead of being all smooshed down like it usually was when she woke up.

"Hey," replied Lauren, scooching herself up to a sitting position and closing the magazine before Chrissy could see the topic of the quiz she'd been taking. She suddenly felt disloyal for starting the quiz, even though it had been just for fun. "It's raining," she said, gesturing to the window.

"Yes, it is," Chrissy yawned. Raindrops streamed down the old glass panes in rivulets, blurring the pink and green of the climbing roses outside the window. "I guess the beach is out of the question. What should we do? Maybe go back to the library? That was awesome," said Chrissy, pulling herself up to a sitting position too and hugging herself around the knees.

Lauren hauled her laptop off of the floor next to her bed, where she'd left it last night, and opened it up. "We could," she said. "Or we could go to the whaling museum. It sounds boring, but it's pretty cool, really." As she said it, Lauren remembered how she had wondered at the beginning of the vacation if Chrissy would think the whaling museum was lame. Now she didn't even worry about that. She knew Chrissy would love it too. And if for some reason she didn't, she definitely would never call it lame. Chrissy might have some strange opinions when it came to boys and romance, but she was definitely enthusiastic and up for trying new things. Lauren realized how much she liked having Chrissy around. It was kind of cool to have a BFF.

Lauren clicked on the weather report. "It's supposed to clear up by early this afternoon. Maybe we can do something this morning and then head to the beach after lunch?"

"Sure," said Chrissy.

"Hey, you left your phone downstairs last night, but I brought it up and plugged it into your charger, in case you wanted to text Justin this morning. But I guess it's too early out in California?"

Chrissy looked down at her knees and swallowed. "Yeah. Well. He hasn't been all that good about replying very quickly lately."

"Oh. Sorry," said Lauren. The two girls sat in silence. Chrissy stared out the window, suddenly looking a little sad. Maybe the weather was bumming her out? Or maybe she was just tired. Lauren was trying to figure out how to bring up Charlie. She decided just to do it. "Chrissy? Can I ask you something?"

There must have been something serious about her tone, because Chrissy immediately sat up straighter and looked at Lauren. "Um, sure."

"Do you . . . like Charlie?"

"Sure I do."

Lauren noticed that she'd answered very quickly. "No, I mean, *like* like him."

"*Like* like him? Charlie? Ew. No."

Lauren felt her face get hot. "What do you mean, 'ew'?"

"Oh, no, I didn't mean 'ew' as in eeeew!" Chrissy said, speaking quickly again. "I just meant, um, that there was no way I would think of him That Way. If I liked anyone better than I like Justin, which by the way I do not, but if I did, I would like Frank. I think he's really cool. Or maybe Matt B. Or even Owen. But definitely not Charlie. Why would you even think such a thing?"

Lauren could see Chrissy was being sincere. She looked hurt. Lauren felt terrible. "I'm sorry, Chrissy. That was a dumb thing for me to ask you. It's just that—well,

Charlie barely looks at me. I think he kind of likes you. He seems to hang around you a lot more often than he does me. So I just wondered if, well, if it was mutual."

"It's not," said Chrissy firmly. "And I really don't think he likes me. He barely knows me. You know what my sister told me? That boys are drawn toward girls who give off vibes that they're not interested. And I am definitely not interested, so if anything, he's just picking up on that."

Lauren nodded. Maybe Chrissy's sister was right. She'd read something about that phenomena. But she was pretty sure that kind of thing mostly applied to older boys, so she couldn't worry about that right now. What she needed to do was get Charlie to spend more time with her. Then he'd realize that she, Lauren, was just like him. It was just a matter of time before he saw the light and realized the two of them were meant to be together.

She decided to change the subject. "So remember I mentioned the big Fourth of July cookout? It's this Thursday night."

Chrissy nodded. "I know. I can't believe it's the Fourth already. What should I wear?"

"That's what I was going to say. People wear anything

from shorts and tees to fancy dresses. There's this awe-some vintage clothing store off Main Street that has the coolest old dresses from the fifties, sixties, and seventies, and it's super cheap. We could use our babysitting money and go there this morning to see if we can find something to wear to the party. I've decided that I can stretch my casual style a little bit for one night and get dressed up! Maybe you can help me choose something that will make me look irresistible to Charlie."

Chrissy looked at her for a minute and looked like she was about to say something, then changed her mind.

"Let's do it!" said Chrissy, flinging back the covers. She hopped out of bed.

Half an hour later Lauren led Chrissy into the vintage clothing store. A bell tinkled as they opened the door. She loved the smell—a combination of old-fashioned per-fume, wood polish, and ocean breezes—which seemed to swirl around the high-ceilinged shop, thanks to the rotat-ing fan overhead.

There were several people inside, and the nice woman behind the register smiled at Lauren, looking as though she recognized her from summers past.

Lauren led Chrissy to the back, where a rack of

dresses lined the entire back wall.

"This place is awesome!" said Chrissy, touching a wild looking straw hat. Its wide brim was festooned with bright blue feathers.

Lauren smiled with delight. It was rare that Chrissy ever thought something wasn't awesome, and Lauren really liked that about her. Lauren always worried about everything, but Chrissy always seemed to think things would just work out. Lauren vowed to try to be more like her.

They tried on several dresses apiece. Finally they both stepped out of the dressing room at the same time, looked at each other, and beamed.

"That is perfect on you!" said Chrissy, jumping up and down and clapping her hands as she gazed at Lauren.

"And that is perfect on you!" said Lauren, shaking her head in amazement at how great her friend looked.

The owner of the shop came around from behind her register and looked at both of them. "Those dresses were made for both of you!" she exclaimed. "I wasn't sure if anyone would be petite enough to fit into them, and along you both came!"

Lauren's dress looked as though it had been fitted by a tailor. It was a short shift from the sixties, and the pattern was blocks of bright colors—pink, yellow, and aqua, on a white background. She looked at herself in the mirror. It really was an awesome dress. It made her look at least a year older, maybe two. And she had the perfect black flats to wear with it.

Chrissy's was from the fifties. It was a delicate rose pink, fitted in the bodice, with thin spaghetti straps, and then it billowed out in a ballerina-like skirt. She did a little twirl in front of the mirror, and her dress spun out in a circle. Lauren thought the soft pink color of the dress made Chrissy's auburn hair look even prettier than usual, and she told her so. Chrissy beamed.

"I'm so glad you are totally abandoning your casual style!" cried Chrissy. "That dress is perfect."

Lauren paused. Oh no. Was this dress a *total abandonment* of her casual style? "Should I not wear a dress?" she asked. "You're right. Charlie is so casual. Maybe I should just wear shorts instead."

"Lauren," Chrissy said with a bit of irritation in her voice, "you look beautiful in that dress. Anyone who sees you will see how beautiful you are in that dress . . . in any dress really. You are not going to wear shorts just because you think some guy would rather see you in shorts!"

Chrissy's voice had gotten louder and she stood there with her hands on her hips.

Lauren blinked. Was Chrissy yelling at her? She wasn't yelling exactly, but she was using that kind of Mom voice like when Mom was trying to make a point. But then Lauren looked in the mirror. The dress was really pretty. Chrissy was right . . . she should buy the dress and wear it.

"You're right," said Lauren. "This is the dress."

"I told you so!" squealed Chrissy. "I can't wait for the party."

"Look!" cried Lauren. "The sun is coming out now. Beach time!"

They paid for their dresses, ran home, and got ready for the beach.

chapter 10

THE BOYS WERE IN THE WAVES, BODYSURFING,
when Lauren and Chrissy arrived at their usual spot.
The waves were high today, and Lauren spotted Charlie
riding in toward the shore, his strong arms propelling him
along, his back tan, and as shiny as a wet seal. It took
huge amounts of self control for Lauren not to stand and
openly gawk at his gorgeousness.

The beach was much less crowded today, most likely
because of the morning rain, but the sand was nearly dry.
A warm breeze blew puffy white clouds across the sun,
which peeked out frequently, bathing them in warmth.
The wind gusted, blowing Lauren's hair across her face,
and Chrissy and Lauren had to make several attempts at
spreading out the large faded blanket, which billowed and
flapped in the breeze. Finally they plopped down on top
of it. Then they helped each other put on sunblock.

"I brought something for us," said Lauren, her eyes sparkling. She pulled the item from her bag and showed it to Chrissy.

"A volleyball!" exclaimed Chrissy. "I wondered why your bag looked so full! I didn't know you played."

"I don't," said Lauren, looking at Chrissy over the tops of her sunglasses.

"Is this another plan of yours?"

Lauren grinned and nodded. "Well, I can't seem to find the right moment for Operation Cell Phone because the guys never seem to be lying on their blankets. They're always in the water or playing sports. So I thought I'd play the game too. The net is free. The guys are in the water. You and I can play. And then maybe they'll come join us."

"I'm a total fail when it comes to volleyball," Chrissy said, looking unsure.

"Me too," said Lauren. "With any luck, the boys won't care how bad we are. They'll just think it's so cool that we're playing in the first place!"

Beach volleyball turned out to be extremely fun. Lauren and Chrissy volleyed the ball back and forth to each other, lunging, diving, and laughing as they fell in the sand. After awhile, Lauren saw the boys approaching out of the corner of her eye. Frank and Charlie stood side-by-side and watched her and Chrissy, arms crossed, grinning.

"Want to play?" Lauren called to them, hoping her tone was just the right combination of casual and friendly.

Frank and Charlie looked at each other and shrugged. But to Lauren's disappointment, Charlie joined Chrissy on her side. Frank became Lauren's teammate. Her heart sank.

Chrissy and Lauren exchanged a look. Then Chrissy blurted out, "Nope. I call we make different teams. Girls against boys."

Frank and Charlie looked at each other and nodded. Frank and Chrissy exchanged places.

"Prepare yourselves for immediate annihilation," said Frank in a Martian-style voice.

Lauren giggled in spite of herself. Frank really was pretty funny, and it was cool the way he wasn't afraid to act goofy.

They began with simply volleying the ball back and forth. At first, Lauren and Chrissy were hopeless. The boys scored point after point, with Charlie announcing the score loudly and pumping his fist every time they made a point. Lauren and Chrissy laughed so hard at how bad they were that Lauren's stomach almost started to hurt. But after a few more volleys, they got into a rhythm. Lauren figured out how to set up a shot for Chrissy, who almost managed to smash it into a place where the boys couldn't reach it. Then Chrissy did the same for Lauren, who jumped high and spiked it just inside the line.

"Nice shot!" called Frank admiringly. The girls had finally scored a point!

Charlie scowled. Lauren guessed he was pretty competitive, and that he wasn't used to losing a point. No wonder he was such a successful athlete.

"Volley for serve!" Charlie called gruffly. He wasn't smiling. He threw the ball up and then slammed a serve across the net. It seared its way down at a blistering speed. Both girls shrieked and jumped out of its path. Charlie grinned. "And that is how you do it!" he yelled to no one in particular. "Our ball!"

The game was lopsided, to put it mildly. But the girls managed to score two more points. The first time they both jumped up at the same time and the ball ricocheted off their arms at a strange angle, clearly unanticipated by the boys, and the ball dropped gently over the net on the boys' side, scoring the point. The second time, Lauren jumped high and slammed it downward as hard as she could.

Charlie lunged for it, trying to hit it back over his shoulder as he laid himself out horizontally. But he couldn't reach it. The ball bounced just a few inches past his outstretched hands.

"Out!" he yelled, his face still in the sand.

Frank looked down at Charlie and tilted his head to the side. "Yo, bro," he said gently. "I think it was in. Or at least on the line."

"No way," said Charlie, clambering back to his feet, sand flying everywhere. "It was *out!*" He said the last word with such force that Chrissy actually flinched. Then he stopped and looked at Frank and looked back at the girls. Then he made a dismissive gesture and said in a sulky voice "Okay. Fine. Their point. It's nineteen to three, us."

The boys ended up winning twenty-one to three. By the time the game was over, the rest of the guys were standing on the sideline, waiting for the next game.

"Nice game!" said Frank. "You guys want to play another one?"

"No thanks!" said Chrissy and Lauren at the same time. Lauren was exhausted and hot and thirsty, but elated that she'd spent so much time facing Charlie across the net.

"Maybe we'll see you later, at the snack bar or something," added Lauren hopefully. She and Chrissy walked back to their blanket and plunked down.

"That was awesome!" breathed Lauren, reaching for her water bottle in her tote bag. She took a long swig, but in her mind she was re-enacting the whole game. "Did you like playing with Frank?"

"I guess so," said Chrissy in a quiet voice.

"Charlie is such an amazing athlete, isn't he?"

"He's an amazing jerk, if you ask me," muttered Chrissy.

Lauren was sure she had misunderstood her. "What did you say?"

"Oh, come on, Lauren! He's such a poor sport! He argued practically every call and he was constantly jumping in front of Frank, hogging shots," Chrissy said, unable to hold back her irritation. "Anyone who is that competitive over a silly beach volleyball game seriously needs to chill out!"

Lauren blinked at her. "I can't believe you said that about him," she said. "He was just being competitive. That's what good athletes do. It's how come they're good athletes."

Chrissy started to say something, but then seemed to

think better of it and said nothing. She pulled out her own water bottle and took a long gulp.

Lauren felt terrible. She didn't want to argue with Chrissy. She knew, deep down, that if Chrissy had a crush who was nearby—instead of thousands of miles away— she'd get it, and understand better where she was coming from. Everything would be so much better if Chrissy would just like Frank already!

"Speaking of good athletes," she said in the most casual tone she could muster. "Frank was pretty good too, don't you think? I bet he's almost as good of an athlete as Charlie is—"

But Chrissy didn't allow Lauren to finish. "Seriously, Lauren?" she interrupted, her cheeks turning red. "Why are you pushing Frank on me again? I've told you I don't like Frank. I like Justin! Justin is my crush, just the way Charlie is yours! I know you have a plan. I know you want the Plan to work. But honestly I'm a little sick of the Plan. It's all you talk about and all you think about. Can't we please, please just talk about something else?"

"I waited the whole year to carry out this plan!" said Lauren angrily. "It's the whole reason to be here this summer! I don't care about anything else!"

Chrissy stood up, her eyes flashing. "Well, thanks. I know you weren't planning on having me here and believe me, now I'm sorry I am here too. And I might not know a lot about boys, but I don't think that the Plan is the way to win anyone's heart. You can't keep trying to be someone you're not. Someone whose every move is dictated by a magazine, and who changes the way she looks and acts to get a guy to notice her. You're great the way you are! Why can't you accept that? And why don't you want a boy to like you for that?" Chrissy took a deep breath and looked down at the sand. In a quieter voice she added, "I'm tired of the way you keep making me hang around with your precious Charlie because he's kind of competitive and stuck up, okay?"

Lauren didn't know what to say. She felt too upset to speak. The two girls stared at each other in stony silence for a few moments.

Finally Chrissy spoke. "I'm sorry. That was mean. I think I'm going for a walk to the pier. I'll be back in awhile."

And she walked off, leaving Lauren alone.

chapter 11

LAUREN SAT ON THE BLANKET, STARING OUT AT
the ocean. The sky had clouded over again. The waves
swelled high, then rolled toward shore and broke with
foamy white water, then receded, leaving shining dark
sand behind. Chrissy was a speck in the distance, but
Lauren could see her, sitting on a jutting-out pier beyond
an outcropping of rocks, maybe half a mile down the
beach. So much for Chrissy becoming her BFF. They still
had almost a week left of vacation. What would happen
now? Would they fight the whole time? Would they be
able to continue sharing a room? Keep up appearances
in front of her parents? This was awful. Her eyes misted
up, and the horizon line blurred in front of her.

Lauren replayed their fight over and over in her mind.
Her thoughts were swimming. Charlie wasn't a jerk. Not
her Charlie. He was perfect. Okay, maybe Chrissy didn't

like him, but that's just because she didn't understand him.

But what if she was a bad friend for concentrating too much on the Love Plan and not enough on Plan BFF? She'd never had a BFF before . . . or even a close friend, if she was really honest. Maybe she was as clueless about being a friend as she was about boys. Chrissy, on the other hand, at least had her sister, who sort of counted as a friend. Chrissy was used to dealing with stuff like this. Lauren was not. Lauren felt a surge of frustration at her parents for not having had any more children. Maybe if Lauren had a sibling, she'd have more experience in dealing with situations like these. Besides, there wasn't a Plan BFF. Chrissy just sort of became her BFF without trying so hard.

"You okay?" asked a voice.

Startled, she turned. It was Frank. He was standing near her, wearing a T-shirt over his wet, too-long blue swim shorts, looking concerned. For the first time, Lauren noticed that he had a sprinkle of freckles across the bridge of his nose, just as she did.

"Yeah," said Lauren. "I think. Chrissy and I kind of had a fight about . . . well, about a bunch of things. She doesn't like the way I've been acting." Had she just shared all this information with him? He was really easy to talk to . . . unlike Charlie, who left her tongue-tied and unsure of herself. Maybe because he wasn't Charlie's caliber. He wasn't so intimidating, so take-your-breath-away gorgeous. He was just Frank. It was really sweet, Lauren realized, that Frank was concerned. Why couldn't Chrissy like him? He really was a great guy. Maybe if Chrissy saw how concerned he was, she would realize how great he was, unlike Justin, who might as well live on Mars, he was so far away.

"It'll be okay," said Frank. "Friends fight sometimes."

"They do?" asked Lauren.

"Well, sure," said Frank. "I get annoyed with my friends a lot. But it all works out in the end."

"Chrissy always thinks things will work out in the end too," Lauren replied.

"Don't you?" asked Frank.

"Not without a plan," said Lauren. "I mean, not a plan but, well, yeah a plan. I think you have to always know what you want to happen."

"That sounds kind of boring," said Frank. "Because if you don't know what's going to happen then you can have all these great surprises."

"Oh, I hate surprises," Lauren said quickly.

"What? How can you possibly hate surprises?" Frank asked.

"Well, they're just so . . . unpredictable . . ." Lauren explained.

"And that's what makes them fun!" Frank said in a teasing voice.

Lauren couldn't help but smile.

"Well, are you going to go try to talk to her?" asked Frank, motioning toward Chrissy.

"Why don't *you* go talk to her?" suggested Lauren. "I bet you can convince her to come back and maybe play another game or something? That was fun, playing volleyball. I had a good time."

"Me too," said Frank, smiling. "But when I walk away like that, I usually want to be left alone. She probably just needs a cool off. I'm sure you guys will work things out."

Lauren sighed. "I'm not sure what to do. I mean, should I go talk to her?"

Frank debated and then shook his head. "Nah. Maybe just wait, and I'm sure she will let you know when she's ready to talk about what happened."

Lauren nodded. That definitely made sense. Frank was pretty smart. "Okay. Maybe I'll read or something and wait for her to come back. Thanks," she added.

"You're welcome," he replied, and headed back over to his friends. "I'll see you later!"

Lauren reached into her bag to grab *Moby-Dick*, and then decided against it. She picked up Chrissy's book, a thriller geared toward kids her age. It looked awesome.

She was immersed in the story when Chrissy returned.

"Hey," said Chrissy, plunking down next to her.

"Hey," Lauren replied, setting the book down. "Hope you don't mind. I started reading your book. It's good."

Chrissy smiled. "I don't mind. Listen, I'm really sorry I said what I said about Charlie. I think I'm just upset about Justin. He hasn't been texting as much lately and well . . . it's just been on my mind."

"It's okay," said Lauren. "I understand. I'm sorry I keep forcing you to hang out with the other guys. You're allowed to make your own choices. I just thought it would be so much fun for the four of us to hang out together. I hope everything is okay with Justin." As she said it, Lauren realized she meant it. She just thought her friend deserved to be with a great guy, like Frank. But maybe Justin was great too . . . even if he was on the other side of the country, and not very good about texting.

"Thanks," said Chrissy, looking relieved. She lowered her head, gesturing with her chin. "The boys have finally settled down. They're lounging. I think that's the first time we've seen them do that since we've been on vacation. Do you want to try Operation Cell Phone? Now might be our one chance!"

Lauren darted a glance at the boys. It was true. It was the perfect opportunity! The awkwardness she had felt with Chrissy was completely gone now, and Lauren felt hopeful, once again, that they could become real BFFs.

"You think we should?" she asked.

"Definitely," said Chrissy. "It's what you've planned for all year. Now or never!"

"Let's do it!" Lauren said excitedly. Maybe, after all these false starts, this would really, truly work.

"Okay. Shall we review the steps?" asked Chrissy, a mischievous look on her face.

Lauren had a sneaking suspicion that Chrissy knew exactly what the steps were, and that she was just teasing her. But Lauren didn't mind. Friends teased each other, after all. She pulled out her index card. The two girls shimmied down onto their stomachs and lay side-by-side, the card between them.

"So, okay," said Lauren. "We start with me pretending to start searching through all our stuff."

"And should I help you look?"

"Definitely. Then I walk over to the boys. I tell Charlie that I've lost my cell phone and that I'm expecting an important call. I'll ask him if I can borrow his phone to call mine."

"But wait, why wouldn't you just use my cell phone?" asked Chrissy. "Why would you bother to ask him for his?"

"Good point," said Lauren, tapping her lower lip thoughtfully. "I made up this plan before I knew you'd be coming with us to the beach house. But that's an easy one. I'll just say that you left yours back at the house, or that you forgot to charge yours."

"Good idea," said Chrissy, nudging Lauren with her shoulder. "But maybe instead of you asking to borrow his phone to call yours, you just ask him to call it? You know, to like get him used to the action of calling you?"

Lauren frowned, her brow furrowed, thinking about that. "Is that a social anthropology tip?" she asked. Chrissy confirmed it was probably something Liz would recommend. "Okay," Lauren said, nodding happily. "That just might work. Good thinking."

"Thanks."

"So I give him my number, he calls my phone, it rings, I pretend to find it, and then I say thanks. Then I chitchat with him about sports or literature."

"Or sportsmanship," Chrissy added with a wink.

Lauren pretended to glare at her and continued. "And then after we've had a real, actual conversation, I'll flirt with him. I'll flirtatiously remind him that he has my cell number now, and then I'll flirtatiously suggest that he text me sometime." She waited for Chrissy to say something.

Chrissy blinked at her. "Oh! Sorry. That's it? That's the whole plan?"

"You don't think it will work?"

"No! I mean, yes! I totally think it will work. Let's roll!"

"Okay. First thing to do is bury the cell phone. I brought a plastic baggie to put it in so it doesn't get ruined under the sand. My parents would totally kill me if I ruined my phone!" Lauren glanced over to be sure the boys weren't watching. Then she pulled the baggie containing her phone from her tote bag and dug a shallow hole in the sand next to her side of the blanket. She placed the phone in the hole, and swept sand back over the top. "Phase one is complete."

"Wait! Question!" said Chrissy.

"What?"

"Why is the phone in the bag? Won't it look like you knew you were going to lose it?"

Lauren thought about that, but then shook her head. "No, I can say I keep it in the plastic baggie to keep it from getting wet!"

"Genius," said Chrissy. "One more question. What should I do while you are having the flirtatious conversation with Charlie? Maybe I should bust out my phone and pretend to be talking to someone?"

Lauren started to nod, and then violently shook her head. "No, you can't do that. Because I'll have just told him that you left your phone back at the house. No, no, that would be disastrous."

"Yeah, true. So maybe I'll just go for a walk or something."

"Sure, sounds good. So . . . phase two is ready to commence. Time for me to start searching for my missing phone," she said.

Chrissy nodded and gave her a subtle thumbs-up.

Lauren sat up and casually reached into her bag. Were the boys looking over this way? She didn't dare look up to find out. She rummaged casually, then grew increasingly concerned. She began taking stuff out of the bag. Chrissy joined in to help. Soon they were both on hands and knees, crawling around on the blanket, shaking out their T-shirts and looking inside all the pouches of their tote bags. A few more minutes of this and then . . .

"Looking for something?"

Lauren jumped. It was Charlie! And Frank. The boys were standing right next to their blanket!

This was not going according to the Plan. She was supposed to approach them! She was so flustered, she forgot if she had even come up with a contingency plan on her flowchart allowing for the possibility of Charlie just showing up like this. She started to panic.

She felt Chrissy nudge her in the ribs. She recovered. "Oh! Hi, you guys. Um, yeah. I seem to have misplaced my cell phone. I can't find it anywhere."

"Wow. That stinks," said Frank. "You want me to call it and see if we can hear it ring?"

"Um, no! I mean, yes . . . but . . ." Lauren stammered. Now she was completely flustered. It was supposed to be Charlie, not Frank, who called her phone! Oh, why was the Plan so hard! Why was Frank always showing up at the wrong time, butting in when his help was not wanted? She gathered herself, made herself think clearly. "I, uh, hate to make you go to the trouble. Maybe you have your phone on you?" she asked Charlie in the most casual voice she could muster.

But Charlie didn't seem to be paying much attention to the drama unfolding before him. He was staring out at the water. "The waves are picking up, dude," he said. "We should go back to bodysurfing."

"He doesn't even have a phone because he keeps breaking them," said Frank with a good-natured roll of his eyes. "But I have mine right here. What's your number?"

Miserably, Lauren recited her phone number for Frank. Loudly enough for Charlie to hear it, just in case he was secretly paying attention . . . and got a new phone, and had it long enough to call her before breaking it.

Frank punched in her number. The four of them stopped to listen for a ring. Then Lauren remembered. She'd forgotten to turn on the ringer. The phone was set to vibrate. There was no way they'd hear it.

"Uh, Laur?" asked Chrissy. "Do you have it set on silent, by chance?

Lauren nodded slowly. "Yes. I guess I do."

"Maybe it got buried in the sand," said Frank. "Charlie, come help us look."

The four of them got down on hands and knees and began feeling around in the sand. Of course, Lauren knew where she'd buried it. But she made sure to kneel down next to Charlie, at the other side of the blanket from where she knew her phone was buried. At one point, their hands touched underneath the sand. A thrill zipped through her. They'd touched! They'd practically held hands!

"Got it!" yelled Frank, triumphantly holding up the plastic bag containing Lauren's phone. "Boy, it was really buried," he said. "Good thing you had it in this bag or it could be totally trashed."

"Thanks," said Lauren numbly, taking the phone from him.

"Let's go, dude!" said Charlie. "The waves are awesome right now!"

"Be right there," said Frank. "I need to put my cell phone back with my stuff."

After the boys had left, Charlie toward the water where their other friends were already surfing, and Frank toward the boys' stuff, Lauren groaned and turned to Chrissy. "That was an epic fail," she said.

"Yeah, it kind of was," agreed Chrissy. "Too bad. I guess neither of us thought to make sure the ringer was activated. Still, it was kind of sweet the way Frank was so willing to help out, don't you think?"

Lauren just nodded, but she wondered if there was more to Chrissy's comment. Did it mean that Chrissy had finally seen the light? Was she thinking about switching her crush? Lauren knew she couldn't ask Chrissy right then and there—given the fact that they had just made up and all that—but she promised herself she'd try and find out more later.

Just then, the phone in Lauren's hand vibrated. Who could that be? She stared down at the caller's number. It was unfamiliar.

"Hello?" she said.

"Hey, Lauren. It's Frank."

She whirled around to look. Sure enough, he was standing near the boys' blankets, on his phone. He looked at her, grinned sheepishly, and waggled his fingers in a small wave.

"Um, hi." She waggled her fingers back at him.

"I was wondering if you want to go have ice cream later," he said.

Lauren tried not to groan into the phone. Was he asking her out? That couldn't be. He must mean with the group. With Chrissy. And Charlie. "Well, um, maybe," she faltered. "Can Chrissy come too?"

"Er, yeah, sure," said Frank.

"So, like, everyone will be there?"

"Yeah, sure," he said again. "Meet at Rudy's? Maybe like at seven?"

"Okay."

"Well, bye."

"Bye."

She hung up. She watched him jog down to the water to join his friends in the waves.

Operation Cell Phone: fail. The Love Plan was doomed.

chapter 12

"DOES THIS MAKE ME LOOK STUPID?" ASKED LAUREN.
She stood before the full-length mirror in front of her closet door, her back to Chrissy, one hand on her hip, the other flicking at the skirt she had on.

In the mirror, Lauren watched Chrissy put down her book, roll over from her back to her stomach, and lie diagonally across the bed. She put her chin in her hands and regarded Lauren, one eyebrow raised.

"No. It does not make you look stupid. You look cute. You looked cute in the last four outfits you tried on too."

Lauren rolled her eyes and turned back to look at herself in the mirror. "I've decided my new personal style philosophy is girly-casual," she said. "Which means I can go supercasual sometimes, but I can also dress things up and be really girly when the situation calls for it. A lot of guys really like girly girls. I think this outfit strikes the right balance, don't you?"

"Lauren, you should wear whatever you feel good in," Chrissy replied.

"So what are you going to wear?" asked Lauren.

Chrissy sat up and stared down at her T-shirt and shorts. "Uh, I thought I'd wear this?" she said.

"But we're going out to Rudy's for ice cream. Frank is going to be there. I think he's a pretty nice dresser, from what I've seen, except for that dorky bathing suit of his."

"I don't care if he's a nice dresser. Because I don't like Frank. I thought I made it clear, I like Justin."

Lauren shrugged, and uncapped her lip gloss. "I get it. I just think it's always smart to keep an open mind." she said, smiling at Chrissy. Chrissy's eyes flashed. "Would you please stop lecturing me on guys?" she replied, struggling to keep her voice even. "I like Justin. Not Frank. If you think Frank is so great, why don't you start liking him?"

Lauren stopped slathering lip gloss and turned around to face Chrissy. "Ew. As if. I like Charlie, in case you forgot."

"Well, maybe you should rethink that," said Chrissy. "Because Frank is much more interesting than Charlie. Have you really not noticed that Charlie is kind of obnoxious? And not really very interesting? If you think

Frank is so fabulous, you should go out with him!"

Lauren shoved her lip gloss back together and then slammed it down on her dresser. "Okay, maybe we should stop talking about this. I like Charlie. You like Justin. I'll stop trying to make you like Frank, and you will stop saying bad things about Charlie. Deal?"

Chrissy sighed. Hadn't they essentially made this same deal at the beach?

"Deal," she said finally.

They walked in silence toward Rudy's. Lauren glanced at Chrissy's casual denim shorts, cute black T-shirt, and neon pink flip-flops, and wished she'd gone that route. She felt stupid and overdressed in her skirt and cropped top and wedge sandals. Like she'd made way too much of an effort.

Her mind was a whirl. What if Chrissy was super-mad at her? What if Chrissy decided to go back to school and tell all their friends about how Lauren had lied about Charlie, that Lauren was not going out with Charlie, nor had they ever been going out? The humiliation would be unbearable. Lauren wondered if she could transfer schools. Didn't kids do that all the time?

The closer they got to Rudy's, the more upset Lauren

felt. This beach vacation had not turned out at all the way she'd imagined.

And deep down, way deep inside her, a tiny voice whispered: *Charlie is kind of a jerk. And Frank is really sweet.* She tried ignoring the voice . . . but it kept going. *Maybe Chrissy is right about Charlie. Remember how he was kind of a bad sport in volleyball? Remember how uninterested he seemed in talking about anything? Maybe he's uninteresting.*

He isn't! She almost said it out loud. The two girls were nearly at Rudy's. Then something Chrissy had said echoed in her mind. *Frank is much more interesting than Charlie.*

Frank?

He was, actually. He was totally more interesting than Charlie. And funnier. And nicer. He was the one who offered to look for the phone and who came over to see if she was okay when Chrissy stormed off.

And in a way, Frank was just as cute as Charlie. Not the tall, athletic physique, broad shoulders, perfect hair kind of cute. But the interesting, funny, quirky good looks, I-don't-care-what-people-think confident kind of cute. Plus, he had those adorable freckles.

Wait a minute. Why was she thinking about Frank? Now she was totally and utterly confused. Did she have a crush on Frank? Or was she still in love with Charlie? She started to panic just as they were walking into Rudy's.

Charlie wasn't there. But Frank was, and so were the two Matts and Owen and Cody and Grant and also three little kids—two girls and a boy. They looked like they might be between four and seven years old. What were they doing there?

"Hey!" yelled Frank, waving wildly at the girls from the large table where they were all sitting. "Over here!"

The girls weaved their way through tables of people eating ice cream, toward their table.

"This is my sister and brother, Isabel and Josh, and that's our cousin, Natalie," said Frank.

"I didn't know you had little brothers and sisters. They're cute," said Chrissy, ruffling Isabel's dark, curly hair.

"We're not cute!" protested Josh.

"And not little!" added Isabel. Then she smiled up at Lauren. "You're pretty. I like your ballerina skirt."

Lauren felt herself blush.

"Charlie isn't coming," said Frank, looking everywhere

but at Lauren. "He had to go somewhere with his family for dinner."

"That's fine!" said Lauren, way too quickly and eagerly.

"My dad gave me money for all of us to get ice cream," said Frank, "since I'm taking my little brother and sister along. What can I get for you?"

"Strawberry frappé with whipped?" said Lauren.

"Double-scoop chocolate chunk and coconut?" said Chrissy.

"Coming right up," said Frank. "If you don't mind watching the little guys."

"We're not little!" shouted Isabel.

"He didn't mean you, silly," said Lauren, scooching herself in to sit at their end of the table. She jerked a thumb in the direction of Frank's friends. "He meant them."

She saw Frank grin before he turned and headed up toward the ice-cream counter.

"I'll go help him carry everything," said Chrissy, and she followed Frank to the counter.

Lauren's brow furrowed. *Great. What if Chrissy suddenly decides to take my advice, and starts crushing on Frank,* she worried. She put that thought out of her mind and decided to focus on the kids. She was pretty good with kids and they were generally a lot easier to talk to. "Who wants me to draw a picture of them?" she said to them.

"Me!"

"Me!"

"Me!"

Lauren picked up the cup of crayons from the table and turned over her paper place mat. "Hold still," she said to Isabel, and began drawing.

Frank and Chrissy returned with their ice cream as she was halfway through drawing Josh.

"You're an awesome artist," said Frank admiringly. He and Chrissy stared down at the drawing of Isabel that Lauren had already finished.

Chrissy didn't say anything. She took a seat down at the other end of the table and pulled out her cell phone to check her messages for what seemed to Lauren like the hundredth time that day. Lauren watched as Chrissy stared at her phone and appeared to read and then reread a text. Then she quickly closed it up again and shoved the phone into her purse. Lauren tried to make eye contact with her, but Chrissy looked down at the floor.

"Everything okay?" asked Lauren, taking a delicious sip of strawberry frappé.

Chrissy nodded quickly. She's definitely still upset with me, Lauren thought, a knot forming in her stomach. Luckily, the little kids had plenty of energy to keep the conversation going, and no one seemed to notice the tension between the two girls.

A little while later, they'd finished their ice cream. The girls said good-bye to the group, thanked Frank for treating them, and headed home. "Looks like things worked out, right?" Frank whispered to Lauren, nodding at Chrissy.

"Oh, yeah, everything's fine," Lauren whispered back. As if.

"See?" said Frank. "Sometimes things just work out."

Lauren and Chrissy barely said a word as they walked home. Lauren tried striking up a conversation a few times, but Chrissy seemed to be a million miles away. They joined Lauren's parents in the sitting room and watched the end of a long, complicated spy movie of some sort. Then they climbed the stairs, got into bed, and turned out the light.

ON WEDNESDAY, THE GIRLS WENT TO THE BEACH
and tried to act as though everything was normal. But
there was definitely tension in the air between them.
Lauren grew more and more worried. At dinner, they
both made an effort at polite conversation, but Lauren
was sure her parents noticed something was wrong.
Luckily, they didn't say anything. The four of them
watched an old movie together, and then the girls went
upstairs and went right to bed. Lauren fell asleep with a
lump in her throat.

Thursday morning Lauren was awakened by a car-
dinal. It sat on the tree branch outside her window singing *prettyprettyprettyprettypretty!* over and over. Sun
streamed in through the parted curtains. She closed her
eyes again and stretched like a cat, savoring the anticipa-
tion of another beach day waiting to happen. And tonight

was the barbecue! It was hard to believe they would have to pack up and go home in two more days.

And then she remembered the fight, and that Chrissy was still mad at her. She realized right then that she had to fix things so they could enjoy the last couple of days of their beach vacation. Chrissy was too important to her— Lauren couldn't let her stay mad. They had to talk things out. She turned to look over at her friend, ready to apologize for everything.

Lauren realized that Chrissy wasn't in her bed and was instantly wide awake.

Two minutes later Lauren charged downstairs and into the kitchen, where her parents were sitting at the table reading the newspaper and drinking their coffee. Lauren was shocked at how calmly they sat there. Why hadn't they called the police? Organized search parties? What if Chrissy was hitchhiking her way back to New York and had been picked up by some crazy person?

"Where's Chrissy?" she asked, panic rising in her throat.

Her mother lowered her coffee cup and gaped at Lauren, still midswallow. Her father, who had just taken a large bite of toast, appeared not to have heard the tone of panic in Lauren's voice. He moved his lower jaw around like a camel at an oasis, chewing his toast. A maddening three seconds ticked by before her mother finished swallowing her coffee and spoke.

"Oh, she was up early! She left a note that she was going out for a run."

"And you let her go?"

Her parents both lowered their newspapers and stared at her.

"Honey," said her dad, "it's not like East Harbor is a high-crime area. You can look at her note. She said she'd run along Crane's beach. There are tons of dog walkers out this early in the morning and virtually no traffic."

"Is everything okay between you girls?" her mom asked gently. "I sensed trouble in paradise."

"Everything's fine," said Lauren. She couldn't look at her mom. She knew her mom didn't believe her. She sighed. "Well, not perfectly fine. We just had a teeny tiny disagreement."

Lauren lowered herself into a chair. Maybe her dad was right. Maybe Chrissy was just going for a jog. They'd been jogging every few days together. But maybe not. Maybe she'd decided she couldn't spend one more minute with Lauren after the way Lauren had acted, and decided to try to make her way back to New York. Would Chrissy do something like that?

"Here's her note," said her mom. "She hasn't been gone very long. I heard her go out about ten minutes before I came downstairs."

Lauren looked at the note:

Hi, Mr. and Mrs. Silver, I'm going for a run. I'll stick to Crane's Beach. Back soon. Chrissy :)

"Why don't you see if you can catch up to her and talk things out?" suggested her mom. "I bet it would feel really good to clear the air."

Lauren looked at her mom. Why was her mom always so right? "Good idea. I'll try to catch up with her," said Lauren, and ran upstairs to change into jogging clothes.

Five minutes later she was jogging toward Crane's Beach. It was a beautiful, breezy morning. She realized today was the Fourth of July. The day of the big barbeque. The only stores open on Main Street were the diner and the coffee shop. But she knew the rest of the stores and restaurants would soon be open too. The Fourth was probably the busiest shopping day of the whole year in this town. In a few hours, Main Street would be thronged with shoppers. She took the steps up toward the beach

two at a time, dashed across the sand toward the water, and stopped. Which way had Chrissy gone? There was a fifty-fifty chance she'd get it right.

She put a hand up to shield her gaze from the sun and looked to the right as far as she could. She saw joggers, dog walkers, a few people strolling and looking for shells and sea glass, but no Chrissy. She looked left. In the far distance, she could see the outcropping of rocks and beyond it, the dock. Wait. Was that a person, sitting on the end of the dock? It was hard to tell if anyone was there, let alone that it was Chrissy, because the sun was shining directly in her eyes. But the pier did seem to be a good spot for brooding. Lauren decided to take the chance and began jogging in that direction.

As she drew closer, she saw that it *was* a person sitting at the end of the pier. A few more steps, and it became clear that the person was Chrissy. Chrissy did not appear to have seen Lauren yet. She sat, dangling her legs over the side of the pier, her arms perched on the rung of the railing, her chin on her arms. She stared out at the ocean.

Chrissy did not turn around as Lauren walked down the pier toward her. Had she heard her? Did she not care? Was she still that mad?

Lauren stopped just behind Chrissy. "Hi," she said in a small voice.

Chrissy turned. Her eyes were shiny. "Hi," she said, and then turned back to look at the water.

Lauren sat down gingerly next to Chrissy. The two sat silently, staring out at the water. Lauren watched a bird strut around on a sleek black rock. Overhead, an osprey glided high above the water and then dove straight down, emerging with a silvery, wriggling fish in its talons. The girls watched it fly off.

"Are you still mad?" asked Lauren in a small voice.

"At you? No. I'm not mad."

Lauren let out a breath of relief. But still, something wasn't right. "I would understand if you were. I'm sorry about being so focused on the Plan and on Charlie. I . . . I really like having you out here this summer. It's been so much fun. I guess sometimes I get so caught up in my plans that I forget to just enjoy things. I realized I've been talking about Charlie all summer and I don't even know much about Justin. So what's he like?"

Chrissy made a choking sound, and Lauren realized she was crying.

"Chrissy? What's the matter?"

Chrissy turned to Lauren, her eyes now brimming with tears. A tear trickled from the corner of her eye down her cheek. "He texted me. Two nights ago. When we were at Rudy's."

Lauren nodded and waited.

"He said . . . he said he met a girl at the beach. A beach back home. In Malibu. And that they're going out now. He broke up with me." She put her face down on her arms and sobbed quietly, her shoulders shaking.

Lauren reached out a hand and placed it gently on her back. She patted Chrissy. Then she pulled her hand away. What should she say? It was so hard to know how to respond. If it were a quiz in *Chic Chick* she would have three options. (A) Should she tell her good riddance, that Justin was probably a jerk for not appreciating what a great thing they had? (B) Should she say oh, don't worry, you'll find someone new really soon? Or (C) Should she just be quiet and supportive? Lauren closed her eyes and shook her head back and forth quickly. Chrissy was right. Lauren was starting to look at everything as a multiple choice quiz. She vowed to stop taking any more of those magazine quizzes, and to start doing and saying what felt right.

"I'm really sorry, Chrissy," she said softly. "That really stinks."

Chrissy raised her head up and smiled wanly at Lauren. "I know, right?" She took a shaky breath. "It's okay. I'll survive. I'm just feeling, well, kind of stupid is all. I've spent the whole summer blabbing to you about my boyfriend, and then it turns out he's not my boyfriend at all. Maybe he never even liked me. You won't tell everyone at school about this, will you?"

Lauren was secretly shocked. Chrissy always seemed so sure of herself, so confident. Did she actually care that much what the kids at school thought? "Puh-lease," said Lauren with a smile. "As if. Don't you remember how nice you were to me when I confessed to you that I barely even knew Charlie, after blabbing about my 'boyfriend' all school year long?"

Chrissy smiled too. "Oh yeah. I forgot about that. Guess we've both been dorks about these guys, huh?"

"Yes, we totally have been," Lauren nodded. And then she made a face and shrugged. Chrissy burst out laughing.

"Laur, can I ask you something?" she asked when she had caught her breath again.

"Of course!"

"Why did you exaggerate so much about Charlie? I mean, I'm not saying I would hold it against you or anything . . . it's just that, now that I know you so well, it seems really out of character for you to make stuff up like that. Why'd you do it?"

Lauren felt her cheeks flush a little bit and she looked away, but she realized she wasn't mad at Chrissy for asking. It was something she had asked herself more than a few times. "Um, well . . . I didn't mean to. I just liked him so much, and I guess I was really hoping something would happen this year, and I kind of slipped when I started talking about him and . . ." her voice trailed off. Lauren cleared her throat and looked up at her friend. "I don't know. I know I didn't ever mean to lie, but I did. All the girls were talking about their crushes. And I didn't think anyone at school would ever like me back. And I knew nobody at school would know Charlie. So it was kind of easy. And I guess maybe I thought it would make me seem more interesting. It was so much fun to talk about. More fun than, like, what books I read, or how I think the whaling museum is really cool. I always want to try to fit in. . . . Totally lame, I know."

"It's not lame at all. I get it," Chrissy said reassuringly.

"Thanks for telling me. I promise your secret is safe with me." Chrissy crossed her fingers over her heart, just like she had done in Lauren's bedroom that first day of vacation, and Lauren knew that her secret was definitely safe with Chrissy. "But Lauren, you are really interesting. And the whaling museum was awesome. You shouldn't be so afraid to talk about the real you or let people get to know you. You're really great just as you are."

Lauren smiled. *That's exactly the kind of advice that* Chic Chick *would give,* she thought. Chrissy had become her new BFF for sure. Her first BFF ever. Lauren realized that even if the Love Plan failed, she still had Chrissy, and that was pretty great. Suddenly she didn't even care as much about the Love Plan. "Do you still want to go to the party tonight?"

Chrissy took a deep breath. "I'm not sure, Laur. Can I think about it?"

Lauren nodded. "Want to jog home together and eat some of my dad's pancakes?"

Chrissy's smile broadened. "Sounds good," she said.

After a pancake breakfast, they packed up and went to the beach for the rest of the morning. Lauren suggested the beach near their house instead of Crane's Beach, and Chrissy smiled and nodded. She and Chrissy needed some girl time, away from the boys. Plus Lauren was in a state of total confusion about everything. Charlie? Frank? Charlie? Frank? She definitely needed time to sort out her true feelings. Lauren read the novel she brought—not *Moby-Dick*—and they talked about everything except boys. They got home by early afternoon, made themselves peanut butter and jelly sandwiches, and ate ravenously.

"The beach always makes me hungry," said Chrissy, licking some jelly off the heel of her hand.

"Me too," said Lauren. "So, have you decided about the party tonight? If you're going to go?"

Chrissy shrugged. "I guess so. I wouldn't want you to go by yourself. Or with your parents. I'm not feeling totally in a party mood, but we did buy those amazing dresses. So, I'll go."

"Great," said Lauren. Then she remembered something. "My grandfather gave me some money for my birthday that I saved for a special occasion," she said. "And I think this is a special occasion. Want to go get mani-pedis for the party?"

Chrissy jumped from her chair, looking almost like

her old self. "Yessssss!" she said. "I'm going fluorescent!"

They both showered, washed their hair, and then walked into town to have their nails done at the one nail salon in the village, which was a few blocks off Main Street, next to the grocery store. True to her word, Chrissy chose fluorescent orange for her toes and fluorescent green for her fingers. Lauren went with periwinkle-blue on her toes and silver on her fingers. For a second she wondered if Charlie would like it. Then she wondered if Frank would. Then she decided she didn't care because she liked it. The girls admired their nails all the way home. Lauren couldn't wait to get dressed for the party.

chapter 14

"WOW!" SAID MRS. SILVER AS FIRST LAUREN AND then Chrissy descended the front stairs. "You both look like movie stars!"

Lauren smiled and tossed her hair back. She did kind of feel like a movie star.

"I could swear you have grown an inch in the past three weeks," marveled her mother. "And look at Chrissy! You look lovely, honey!"

Chrissy stepped off the last step and did a little pirouette, her full skirt spinning in a wide circle.

Lauren was encouraged by Chrissy's upbeat behavior. She'd been fine at the nail salon, but then once they got home she seemed to be sinking back into her sadness. Lauren caught her checking her phone a few times. Was she looking for a text from Justin? Lauren thought about asking her if she wanted to talk, but then she realized that

Chrissy would come to her if she needed to talk. Chrissy knew she was there for her. So Lauren gave her friend some space. As the afternoon wore on, Chrissy's mood seemed to improve. And now she was pretty much back to her normal, happy self.

Lauren's dad was regarding them from the sitting room off to the right of the stairs. He put down his book, took off his glasses, and massaged his temples, as though he couldn't believe what he'd just seen. "I remember taking you to this party a few years ago, and we spent the whole time swinging on the swing set," he said to Lauren. "You were sound asleep by the time the fireworks started. Slept through all that booming. And now look at you! All grown up!"

Lauren laughed and rolled her eyes for Chrissy's benefit, but she was secretly pleased at the big fuss her parents were making.

Lauren's parents were already dressed for the party. Her mom looked great, wearing a pretty aqua-colored tunic over white pants, with white high heels. Her hair was up in a cool twist, and Lauren could tell that she had taken some extra care with her makeup. Her dad, however, was another story. On top he had on a Hawaiian shirt, which wasn't the best choice in his closet if you asked Lauren, but at least it was festive. His pink Bermuda shorts, on the other hand, were almost too awful for words. "Um, Dad . . . ?" she said, pointing in horror at his shorts as he stood up from his chair.

"What's the matter? Not crazy about my shorts?"

"Um. Not exactly," said Lauren.

"Don't worry. You girls can go to the party ahead of us," he said with a chuckle. "We'll stick with the grown-up crowd and you can pretend you don't know us."

Chrissy and Lauren exchanged a look.

"Okay, we'll walk," said Lauren. She linked arms with Chrissy and headed for the door.

As soon as they were outside, Lauren let out a groan. "Did you see my dad's pink shorts? Did I mention that they're pink?"

"I think he looks . . . nice," Chrissy replied diplomatically.

"Whatever," said Lauren. And then both girls dissolved into giggles.

The beach club was a ten-minute walk from the house. As they approached the large sprawling building, they could see that the wide patio overlooking the beach was already crowded with people. As the girls walked around to the ocean side, they could hear music playing—old-fashioned swing band kind of music—and see twinkling white lights festooning the patio area.

Music played, glasses clinked, people talked and laughed. Most of the grown-ups were dressed up. Several little kids dashed through the crowd and onto the beach, playing tag or something. White-shirted caterers passed trays of colorful hors d'oeuvres.

Lauren scanned the crowd. Was he here? *Oh my goodness,* she thought. She was looking for Frank, not Charlie. She suddenly didn't really care if she saw Charlie. It was all so confusing. How quickly she'd changed her mind about everything. Should she follow her gut and acknowledge to herself that her major crush had shifted from Charlie to Frank? If so, she needed to find Frank. And revise the Plan. She would need to give him her e-mail address or some way to get in touch with her after she'd gone back home. She remembered that he didn't live far away. Just two towns over from her. The high schools in their towns played each other in sports all the time! It was totally possible that they could remain . . . in touch for the rest of the summer, even after they'd gone back home. Lauren realized, with a secret smile to herself, that she had learned a lot about Frank this summer. And Charlie . . . well, what had she learned so far that she didn't already know? Not much. He wasn't exactly an open book the way Frank was.

"Hey," said a voice. Chrissy and Lauren turned. It was Charlie.

Lauren's breath caught in her throat, almost from force of habit. What wouldn't she have given for this moment just a few weeks ago? And now she didn't even care that much. He really was drop-dead gorgeous. He even had dimples when he smiled! And he was smiling. Wait, was she wrong? Did she still like him?

A little kid chasing another little kid bumped into Charlie.

"Oof!" said Charlie, taking a step forward so as not to fall over.

"Sowwie!" said the little kid, and kept running.

Charlie muttered something and shook his head.

"Wait, what did you say?" asked Lauren, sure she hadn't heard right.

"I said, 'I hate little kids,'" said Charlie. "They're just so annoying."

"Oh!" Lauren and Chrissy exchanged a look. "I thought you loved little kids," said Lauren. "I thought I—um—saw you once and you were letting a bunch of kids bury you in the sand."

"Oh, that," scoffed Charlie. "Yeah, that was a one-time thing. My sister begged me to take over her babysitting gig one day because she wanted to go to a concert. So I charged her and the parents. Got paid double. Plus, I kept the ice-cream money the parents had given me for the kids. Still wasn't worth the hassle. I hate babysitting."

Lauren felt a little sick to her stomach. It reminded her of the time she'd found her tooth in her mom's dresser drawer. The one she'd thought had been taken by the Tooth Fairy. It was a bad feeling—even at that time, she had known, deep down, that her mom had been the one to take it and leave money under her pillow, but somehow, facing the stark, honest truth in the form of her tooth in the drawer had been hard to deal with anyway. It was like that with Charlie now. She realized now that she'd known for a long time, on some level, that he wasn't the guy she had fantasized he was. Even so, she decided to test him more, to prove to herself even further that she'd been wrong about him.

"So remember last summer when you were walking in the dunes?" she blurted out. She didn't care if she was bringing up a random subject and if that made her seem totally lame to Charlie, or if it made her seem like a stalker. She wanted to know.

Charlie looked at her, a foggy expression on his face.

"It was near Crane's Beach, but in the restricted zone where all the signs say 'keep out.' I saw you walking around in there. Were you, like, allowed to be there because you were in the Youth Conservation Core or something?"

Charlie nodded slowly as he realized what Lauren was talking about. "Huh? Oh, right. Um, I dunno. I was probably just looking for my lost lacrosse ball. I always accidentally whack it into there."

"Didn't you see the sign that the area was restricted?" Lauren asked, her voice rising a little bit. "Why would you play lacrosse near there?" she demanded.

Charlie just shrugged, clearly annoyed by Lauren's grilling. "I didn't think anyone saw me. Anyway, who cares?"

All at once Frank was there. He'd somehow approached without Lauren noticing. Her heart suddenly began thudding so loudly she wondered if the others could hear it.

"Hey," said Frank. "You guys look awesome."

Lauren and Chrissy both smiled. "Thanks," they said at the same time. Lauren couldn't help but note to herself that Charlie hadn't bothered to compliment them on being dressed up. Had he even noticed? But Frank had. Lauren wondered if he was just being nice or if he really noticed her dress. She glanced up at him.

Frank was as dressed up as Lauren had ever seen him. He had on a royal blue polo shirt and khaki shorts. For the first time, Lauren noticed that he had beautiful, dark blue eyes, the color of the sky on a perfect summer evening. How had she not noticed that before? She tried to get up the nerve to tell him how nice he looked but all of a sudden her heart was going pitter patter and she felt hot.

"So I heard you got busted today," said Frank to Charlie.

Charlie grinned. "Yup. But my mom'll get over it. She always does." He noticed Lauren's quizzical expression. "She's always forcing me to read, read, read. Says I don't do enough of it."

"But I thought you were a big reader," said Lauren. "We always see you reading a big, thick book."

"Yeah, that's how I got busted," he said with a grin. "I made a cut-out inside the book that perfectly fit my MP3 player. So I was actually watching movies when it looked like I was reading. Unfortunately, she found that out this morning when she was cleaning my room."

"So—you don't really like to read much?"

"Psssh. Hate it. Give me a good video game any time."

The music changed from jazzy to slow. The song was an oldie, but the tune was familiar to Lauren. Maybe she'd heard her dad, or even her grandfather, playing it. The band was good; there were at least a dozen musicians, playing brass instruments, saxophones, drums, even a big double bass. A couple of them looked young—possibly even her age.

"These guys are amazing," remarked Frank. Lauren nodded in agreement.

A sob escaped from Chrissy as the slow song played. She put a hand to her mouth and ran from the patio, toward the darkened beach.

Lauren and the boys stared after her.

"What's wrong with Chrissy?" asked Frank, watching

her walk away. "Did I say something to upset her?" He seemed genuinely perplexed.

"No, it's not you. She and her boyfriend broke up," said Lauren. "He texted her the news . . . can you believe that? She's still pretty upset. I'm guessing that might have been their special song or something."

Charlie pumped his fist in the air. "Yessssss!" he said.

Lauren glared at him. "You're happy that she's upset?"

"Naw, I'm happy she's available," he said. "I might have to ask her for her number."

So Charlie did like Chrissy. And now Lauren was sure she was over him because this news didn't make her feel sad at all. But it did annoy her! Couldn't he see that Chrissy was hurting?

"Um, bro, now might not be the right time. She looked pretty upset," said Frank. He looked expectantly at Lauren, who continued to glare at Charlie. How could he be so insensitive? Lauren looked away from Charlie and watched helplessly as her friend made her way through the crowd.

"I'm not sure how to help her," Lauren admitted. "Do you want to try?" she said, turning to Frank.

"Um, I guess I'll go talk to her," Frank mumbled finally, and he headed toward Chrissy, who had almost reached the beach.

Lauren and Charlie were now alone, awkwardly standing next to each other. Lauren couldn't think of much to say. And Charlie seemed to have nothing to say. She was relieved when the Matts approached Charlie and dragged him off toward the food table. She went over to the bar area and hopped up onto a stool. She could see Frank and Chrissy standing on the beach, alone, the sun setting romantically behind them. They seemed to be talking easily to each another. Frank was gesturing dramatically with both hands as he told Chrissy some sort of story. Then Chrissy doubled over laughing.

Did Chrissy and Frank like each other now? Lauren groaned. She'd been trying for this all summer! If they ended up together, it was all her fault!

chapter 15

LAUREN SWIVELED AWAY FROM WHERE CHRISSY
and Frank were standing, so she wouldn't have to watch
how much fun they were having together. She turned
toward the band. They were playing another slow, sad
sounding song. It perfectly suited her mood.

Her dad and mom passed by and she did her best not
to flinch as her gaze flickered over his pink shorts.

"Having fun, honey?" asked her mom.

She managed a smile. "Yeah. The party is awesome."

"Be home by ten, okay, sweetheart?" said her dad.

She nodded. She watched her mom and dad clasp
one another and begin dancing, their bodies swaying in
perfect sync to the music, their cheeks close together.
Her dad whispered something in her mom's ear, and her
mom giggled.

Lauren closed her eyes and shook her head. Even

old people were having a more romantic summer than she was.

"Hey."

Lauren turned around. Chrissy was sitting on the stool next to her.

Now it was Lauren's turn to have her eyes brimming with tears. "Hey," she said.

"What's wrong, Laur?" Chrissy put a hand on her arm and leaned toward her, genuine concern on her face. "Is it me? I know I've been really insensitive about all the Charlie stuff, and I'm sorry I blew my stack about Frank. I've just been really stressed out about Justin. I think I knew for a while something was off, and that was probably making me really cranky. I'm totally sorry."

Lauren couldn't speak. She just shook her head.

"Look, Frank told me about what Charlie said. I swear, Lauren, I don't *like* like him. I never gave him any reason to think I liked him. He's kind of boring and stuck up, and he was so competitive at our volleyball game. No offense. I know you like him. But I swear—"

"I don't like Charlie anymore," said Lauren flatly. "I realized that I like Frank. And Frank likes you. And who could blame him, because you are so totally amazing! And

I think you like Frank. Which isn't your fault because I've been telling you to like Frank since we got here. And now you do like him, and so now you're probably going to hate me for liking who you like."

Chrissy's eyes widened. "No! I so don't!"

"I saw the way he was making you laugh and stuff. Just now. On the beach."

"Yeah, I like him, sure, but I don't *like* like him."

"You're just saying that. Why wouldn't you *like* like him? He's awesome." Lauren had never felt more miserable.

"Lauren." Chrissy put a hand over Lauren's and stared deeply into Lauren's eyes. "You are right that Frank is awesome. But you are wrong about Frank liking me—I guarantee it. You should talk to him. And anyway, the reason I came over to talk to you is that I wanted to point out the saxophonist in the band. After Frank left I walked back here to look for you, and then I spotted him. He had a solo in the last number. Have you ever, ever, in your whole life, seen anyone as cute and amazing as he is?"

Lauren looked. There were three saxophonists, but it was clear which one Chrissy was talking about. He was the youngest by far. Probably just a few years older than they were. He wore a T-shirt, jeans, and sneakers. He wasn't tall, like Charlie, but he was perfectly proportioned, his arm muscles flexing as he played. And he could play. The song they were playing at the moment was a jazzy dance number, and as the girls looked at him, the boy broke out into a solo, his fingers flying up and down the instrument, his saxophone singing out in a sultry melody.

Lauren blinked. "Ah," was all she could say.

"And guess what? I think he smiled at me a little while ago when he wasn't playing," said Chrissy breathlessly. "I think I might go talk to him at their next break."

"You totally should," said Lauren.

"You think?" Chrissy asked, her cheeks flushing in a way that made her look even prettier than usual.

"Absolutely! Go for it!" Lauren cheered. "You know . . . we could come up with a plan . . ." Then she stopped. Chrissy looked at her and rolled her eyes.

Lauren laughed. "And the plan should be that when the song is over you just go over and talk to him and be yourself."

As if on cue, the band members finished the song. All the people on the dance floor clapped and cheered for them. The main guy announced that they'd be taking a short break, and then the band members began folding their music, laying their instruments across their chairs, standing, stretching. A DJ put on a contemporary song, but most people left the dance floor and headed toward the food table.

Lauren gave Chrissy a tiny shove, and Chrissy jumped down from the stool. "What should I say? I mean, what kind of icebreaker should I use? Should I tell him I play the piano, or does that sound dorky?" Chrissy asked.

Lauren grinned at her friend and gave her the same advice Chrissy had been giving her all summer. "Just go be yourself! Someone once gave me that very good advice."

Chrissy grinned back and squeezed Lauren's hand. Then she confidently strode through the crowd toward the band area. Lauren sat, smiling. She was really happy for her.

"Lauren! Lauren! Lauren!" shrieked a pair of little-kid voices.

She looked down. Bobby and Kyle Claussen were standing in front of her. She hopped off the stool and knelt down to give them both a hug.

"When are you going to come back to babysit us?" demanded Kyle. "You are our favortetest babysitter!"

Bobby didn't wait to hear her answer. "Come play with us!" he shouted, jumping up and down.

Lauren allowed the two boys to take her by the hands and drag her away from the patio and over to an area on the sand where kiddy tables were set up. On the tables platters of cheese sandwiches, carrot sticks, grapes, and juice had been laid out.

A few minutes later, Lauren had kicked off her shoes and was deeply immersed in a three-way game of paddle ball with Bobby and Kyle. Chrissy raced up to her, her eyes shining.

"Okay, how'd it go?" asked Lauren, lunging for the ball and returning a lob to Kyle, who let it drop in front of him. "Game!" she said, laughing, and handed her paddle to the boys.

Chrissy clasped her arm. "His name is Kenny," she said, "and he's thirteen—almost fourteen, actually—and that makes him a prodigy because he is soooo good on the sax! Did you hear him? And guess what." She didn't wait for Lauren to guess. "He lives like, five miles away from my house. He and Frank are from the same town. They go to the same school and are actually friendly. And he's totally cool, and smart, and we exchanged numbers, and he's going to call me when we get home and oh, Lauren! He's just amazing!"

Lauren beamed. "That's so great, Chrissy."

"Do you mind if I go hang out with him? He finishes at nine because after that they're doing the fireworks but who cares about fireworks. I can go hang out with him while he has something to eat and then meet up with you right before we have to leave. Would that be okay?"

"Of course that would be okay!" said Lauren. She was trying hard to be cheerful for her friend. "I'm really happy for you, Chrissy."

Chrissy gave a little squeal, bounced up and down a few times, and dashed away. Then she ran back and grabbed Lauren's hand. "I know it wasn't part of the Plan, Lauren, but if you like Frank then maybe you should go tell him."

"Tell him?" Lauren yelped.

Chrissy laughed. "Okay, maybe not *tell* him, but go talk to him. He's really great."

"Well . . . maybe," said Lauren. "I'll try to find him."

"Okay," said Chrissy. "We'll meet up later. I can't wait to tell you everything!"

Lauren grinned. She couldn't wait to hear it.

Lauren picked up her shoes. The warm sand felt nice on her feet. She walked down the beach, a little bit away from the party. The music faded behind her. The darkness swallowed her up and she stood, staring out at the waves rolling in. The white foam reflected off the moon, making it look as though it were glowing. She swallowed back a huge lump in her throat. Of course she was happy for Chrissy. But she felt like the only girl on Earth not to find true love. She'd spent nearly three whole weeks— well a whole year and three weeks—chasing after a guy who didn't deserve it, and meanwhile, she'd let her real crush, Frank, slip away. Why had she been so dense? How could she not have seen him for the awesome guy that he was? And now they would be leaving in two days. And she'd probably not see him again until next summer. She was totally repeating her pattern from last summer, crushing on a guy who barely knew she was alive.

She didn't feel like staying for the fireworks. She wondered if she could text Chrissy and just ask her to meet her at home.

Her phone vibrated deep in the pocket of her dress. She pulled it out. It was an unknown number.

"Hello?" she said cautiously.

"Were you going to leave without saying good-bye?" said a boy's voice on the other end.

"Who's thi—is this Frank?"

"Turn around and find out!"

Lauren spun around. Frank was standing ten feet behind her, his phone to his ear. With his free hand he gave her a little wave and walked toward her.

She closed her phone. Stared at him. He looked nervous. Uncertain. Not like his usual confident, goofy self.

"How did you get my number?" she asked, suddenly tongue-tied herself.

He shrugged. "You had me call you that day you lost your phone, remember? I saved it. Of course. The phone number of a pretty girl is not the kind of thing a dude lets get away."

They stood, staring at each other. Lauren had a million things she wanted to say, but she couldn't get her voice to work.

"I just wanted to tell you before you left that it was fun getting to know you this summer," Frank said, his words tumbling out quickly. His gaze had dropped to the sand. "I just, um, thought, maybe we could keep in touch."

Say something, her inner voice said to her fiercely.

Say. Something. Be casual. Be witty. No, that was the kind of confusing advice *Chic Chick* would give her. Lauren took a breath. What did she *want* to say? "That would be nice," she said, her voice all trembly. "I'd like that. Should I, um, give you my e-mail address?"

"No," he said.

She felt crushed. Should she not have said that?

He stepped toward her. He showed her the screen on his phone:

Lauren ♥

"I don't need your e-mail address 'cause I've got your number."

Lauren felt her face flush as Frank took one step closer and finally looked up, grinning in the most shy and adorable way.

This vacation was going to have the perfect ending after all. The Plan had worked. It didn't work the way she thought it would with the guy she thought it would, but it worked with the right guy. She smiled to herself. It turned out the Plan was foolproof. There was just one minor change she'd need to make to the end of the Plan with the heart at the bottom of the flowchart to make it perfect:

Frank + Lauren = TLF

She couldn't wait to tell Chrissy later. But right here, right now, all she wanted to do was enjoy the moment, and wonder at the way sometimes things really do work out okay in the end . . . even without a plan.

ANGELA DARLING was nicknamed "The Love Guru" by her friends in school because she always gave such awesome advice on crushes. And Angela's own first crush worked out pretty well . . . they have been married for almost ten years now! When Angela isn't busy watching romantic comedies, reading romance novels, or dreaming up new stories, she works as an editor in New York City. She knows deep down that *every* story can't possibly have a happy ending, but the incurable romantic in her can't help but always look for the silver lining in every cloud.

Here's a sneak peek at the next book in the series:

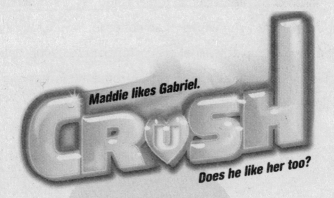

Maddie likes Gabriel.

Does he like her too?

Maddie's Camp Crush

"MOM, YOU WERE SUPPOSED TO TURN LEFT, NOT right!" Maddie Jacobs said impatiently as her mother turned down a lonely looking dirt road.

"Recalculating," announced the cool computer voice of the GPS.

"See? I told you!" Maddie said.

Mrs. Jacobs brushed a strand of brown hair from her face. "I'm just doing what the stupid machine told me to, Maddie," her mom explained in a voice filled with frustration.

"Actually, that is not what the stupid machine told you to do," Maddie pointed out. "By the time we get to camp, the season will be over!"

Her mother gripped the wheel. "Maddie, I'm doing my best, okay? Just let me concentrate."

Maddie leaned back in her seat and resisted the urge to make another comment. Mom had been such a mess since Maddie's father died in the fall. Losing Dad had been hard on everybody, but her mom just didn't seem to be getting any better. It sounded harsh, but sometimes Maddie wished she would just get it together already.

Sighing, Maddie turned to look out the window. Camp was an hour and a half away from home, in the woods of Pennsylvania. The roads were lined with green trees, and the sky above was a perfect July blue. But looking at the familiar scenery only made Maddie feel sad.

When Dad was alive, the trip to camp had been one of the most fun parts of the whole summer. Dad would sing songs that he'd learned at camp when he was a kid, and he'd roll down the windows and they'd all sing along with him loudly. Then he'd make corny jokes about camp, and even though he told the same ones every year, Maddie would still crack up.

"Why did the camper put a snake in the other camper's bed?" Dad would ask, and Maddie would pretend she didn't know the answer.

"Why?" she would say.

"Because she couldn't find a frog!" Dad would finish, and he and Maddie would laugh while her mom rolled her eyes—but she was always smiling.

Then when they got to camp, he would give Maddie the biggest, tightest good-bye hug ever, and he would even pretend to cry, making all her camp friends laugh. In truth Maddie was always a little sad when her parents left, but she never missed them for long because her dad always left a funny note hidden somewhere that Maddie would find—under her pillow or tucked in her slipper or even in the pocket of her bathrobe. Her throat tightened as she thought about the fact that there wouldn't be a note this year. She started to tear up, and she turned to the window to make sure her mom wouldn't see her.

After a deep breath, Maddie glanced at the clock. It was 11:03, and she started to feel anxious. Check-in had started an hour ago, and the girls who checked in first got to pick their beds first. If she didn't get to sleep near Liza, Libby, and Emily, her best camp friends, it would be terrible.

I'll probably end up with a bed next to the shower or the bathroom or something, she thought gloomily.

Liza had said she would try to save her a bed, but they weren't supposed to do that, so Maddie was sure she'd be stuck. She wouldn't be surprised, considering how things had been going wrong ever since last night. After Maddie had packed her duffel bag with everything she needed for six weeks of summer camp, her mom realized that she couldn't lift it and drag it down the stairs to the car. That had never been a problem for Dad. He would always hoist it high over his head and say, "Oof, Mads, what did you pack, brick bathing suits?"

So this morning Mom had called Mr. Donalty from next door and he'd put the bag in the car for them. He was really nice about it, but the whole thing made Maddie miss her dad even more. Besides that, Mom had forgotten to make her special going-away breakfast. Dad had always made her French toast or pancakes.

"Eat up, Mads," he'd say. "You're going to be eating that icky camp food for weeks!"

All Mom had said this morning was, "Are you hungry?" Maddie had answered no, but Mom handed her a bagel as they left the house.

Now she snuck a look at her mother, who was leaning

close to the steering wheel and gripping it tightly. She knew that Mom hated driving far from home, but she didn't accept Uncle Jay's offer to drive them up this year. Maddie wasn't sure why, but her Mom had been funny about accepting help from anyone lately.

Maddie's thoughts shifted to her camp friends, Liza and Libby and Emily. They'd come to the funeral last fall, but that whole thing was a blur. Maddie had been texting them all year long, but it wasn't the same as seeing them in person. She couldn't wait until they could all hang out together, laughing and talking like they always did. Just as long as they didn't want to talk about her dad. . . . She didn't care if Libby told that story about when the possum surprised her in the bathroom that one summer, even though Libby had told it a million times already. She'd rather talk about anything but her dad.

"Camp is going to be good for you, Maddie," her mom had said when Maddie had talked about skipping it this year. "It'll take your mind off things."

Maybe Mom was right, Maddie thought. The excitement of seeing her camp friends again was a really good feeling, a feeling she hadn't felt in a long time.

"Recalculating," announced the GPS again.

"*Mom!*" Maddie yelled, and her mother jumped in her seat.

"Don't yell while I am driving, Madeline!" she yelled back.

Maddie pouted quietly while her mom made another turn. Finally, Maddie saw the familiar sign down the road to the right: CAMP WIMOWAY ENTRANCE A.

"Finally!" Maddie cried, and a look of relief came over her mom's face as she turned down the narrow winding road to camp.

The tree-lined road emerged into a clearing of rustic wood cabins. Cars filled the parking lot as parents dropped off their campers, but Maddie didn't recognize any of them . . . because they were all boys!

Maddie and her mom exited the car, confused. A male counselor wearing a red Camp Wimoway shirt approached them.

"Here for drop off?" he asked.

"Yes," Mrs. Jacobs replied, anxiously looking around. "She's in the Hannah bunk this year."

Camp Wimoway was divided into a boys' camp and

a girls' camp, and each camp was divided into bunks, or cabins. In the girls' camp the bunks were named after former counselors from a long time ago: Hannah, Sarah, Betty, and Gail.

"We've rearranged camp this year," the counselor informed them. "We sent out a map and a note, but some parents didn't get them, I'm afraid."

Mom looked a little guilty. *Great*, Maddie thought. *More changes.*

"You should have gone to Entrance B," the counselor explained. "It's about a quarter mile down the road and then you make a left." Mrs. Jacobs took a little notebook from her purse and he started to draw a map for her.

Maddie remembered that Entrance B led to the camp where the "baby" camp division was—the camp for kids who were, like, six to eight years old. And now that was where the girls' camp was? How embarrassing! Why couldn't Mom have read that e-mail? She started to slink back into the car before anyone noticed she was in the wrong place, but curiosity took over and she looked around at her old camp once more. It was weird to think that the boys were now living where the girls used to live.

A mom and dad walked past with a crying little boy, and Maddie knew how he felt. She had cried her first year in camp too. She looked at her cabin from last year and saw a couple of the boys her own age hanging around on the steps: Jared and Evan. They both looked so much taller than they were last summer! Then Brandon walked up to them. He lived only one town over from Maddie back home, and they had taken a tennis class together in the spring. He nodded at her, half-waving, and she looked away.

He's probably wondering why I'm standing in the middle of the boys' camp like a loser, she thought, and then she turned to open the car door, eager to become invisible before anyone else noticed her.

The sound of a voice coming from a nearby bunk made her pause. It was a boy's voice, a really cool, deep voice with a British accent. She turned slightly and saw a boy about her age—a boy with the most beautiful face she had ever seen.